THE BEAST WITHIN ME

The WOLVES of WHARTON
Book Two

BEAU LAKE

4 Horsemen
Publications, Inc.

The Beast Within Me
Copyright © 2021 Beau Lake. All rights reserved.

4 Horsemen
Publications, Inc.

4 Horsemen Publications, Inc.
1497 Main St. Suite 169
Dunedin, FL 34698
4horsemenpublications.com
info@4horsemenpublications.com

Cover by Battle Goddess Production
Typesetting by Michelle Cline
Editor Vanessa Valiente

Library of Congress Control Number: 2021936529

Print ISBN: 978-1-64450-217-4
Audio ISBN: 978-1-64450-215-0
Ebook ISBN: 978-1-64450-216-7

TABLE OF CONTENTS

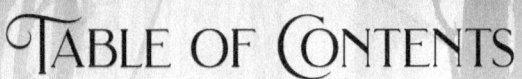

I. 1946

CHAPTER 1
(???)

⊲◆▷

G reta is a small woman who works at the dry cleaner on Jefferson Avenue. She is a bottle blonde, her roots nearly black. Her uniform is a crisp pink pinafore cinched tight over a robin egg blue dress, and her heels tip-tap on the geometric linoleum as she walks.

She often hums as she operates the till, the melody indecipherable. "Here you go, sir," she says, handing me a yellow slip of paper. "Your shirts will be clean and pressed by tomorrow afternoon."

"Thank you, Miss Thorpe," I say, flashing her a smile. I linger at the counter. She smells so lovely: a diaphanous mixture of chamomile and rose. Beneath it, there's something a little more tantalizing. My mouth waters. It's an almost painful feeling—this *wanting*. It's a sharp knife on the back of my tongue. "Say," I continue, "what are you doing tonight?"

Her cheeks turn a deep crimson, and she averts her

eyes. "I don't know," she says. "I expect I'll just head home. I have an early shift tomorrow." She looks up at me through her dark lashes. "Why?"

"Because I'd like to take you out," I reply.

"Really?" Greta's hair is coiled into a chignon at the base of her skull; she tucks an errant strand behind her ear. She pushes her glasses up her long, slender nose.

"Is that a 'yes'?" I ask.

"I'd be delighted," she finally says. "I get off in an hour."

"I'll be back to pick you up." I rap my knuckles on the counter, flashing her a toothy grin. Outside, the air is hot and dense. I stride across the street and into Hart's Drugstore, settling on a stool at the soda fountain.

The soda jerk, a young man with acne dotting his cheeks, wipes his hands on his apron. "What can I get you?" he asks. I recognize him. He's Gerry Calhoun, the son of the local mechanic. Gerry rests his elbows on the counter, surveying me.

"Just a Coca-Cola," I reply. I swivel on my stool and look out the window. From here, I can see the dry cleaner's storefront. I squint and can see Greta inside. I watch as she adds a canister of petroleum dry cleaning solvent into the drum of the washing machine, standing on tiptoes to turn it on. I imagine the rumble of it, the way it fills the small building with its own self-contained atmosphere of overheated air.

Will it affect the way she tastes? Is it like steaming a ham?

Gerry places an icy glass of cola on the countertop, the ice cubes tinkling therein. I place a nickel in his outstretched hand. "Enjoy," he says. "Let me know if you need anything else."

"Sure thing," I reply, but I only have eyes for Greta. I take a sip of my drink, the effervescence tickling my tongue.

Across the street, Greta leans against the counter, examining her nails. She reaches under the counter, pulling out a nail file. *I wonder whether she's humming and thinking of me.*

I am feeling impatient. I glance at the clock.

Finally, Greta turns off the lights, flipping the placard from OPEN to CLOSED. I slide off my stool, sucking the last dregs of my cola through my straw. Giving the soda jerk a nod, I head back out onto the street.

Sweat prickles beneath my arms as the humidity envelops me. I curse at my decision to wear a light button-down; the moist, yellowish patches will be noticeable.

Greta notices me approaching and waves. She waits for a car to pass, then trots across to meet me. "So, where are we going?" she asks, smiling. She holds her clutch in both hands, fiddling with the clasp. *She's nervous.*

"Maybe we could have a drink at The Dock?" I suggest.

"Sure," she replies. "I'd like that." Gentlemanly, I offer her my elbow, and she rests her palm on my forearm. Her hand is soft and cool.

The Dock is only two blocks away, and we walk in companionable silence. I watch her out of the corner of my eye. Her cheeks are a rosy pink, and she casts furtive glances at my face. I catch her eye, making her blush all the more. She looks away, pretending to be interested in the passing cars and pedestrians. She says hello to familiar faces: Mr. James, the mail carrier: Mr. Divita, the pharmacist; and various women she plays cards and board games with like *Make-A-Million* and *Mr. Ree*.

The Dock is relatively busy. We find a small table and settle in. Greta orders a Pink Lady and sips it; the egg whites cling to her upper lip, and I wipe them away with my thumb. "Care to dance?" I ask as the jukebox starts to play a Glenn Miller song.

"Here?" Greta laughs. "No one dances here."

She's right. The Dock is a hole-in-the-wall at best, a far cry from Texaco Star Theater. There's hardly room to walk, let alone cut a rug.

"Come on," I wheedle, "it'll be fun." I take her hand, pulling her close.

Together, we sashay from side to side. At first, she is taut like a guitar string, waiting to be plucked. But soon, she relaxes, allowing me to spin and dip her. The patrons of the bar watch us curiously: some laugh while others raise their drinks in silent salute.

When the song ends, Greta and I return to our table. We both giggle like children, euphoric and embarrassed by our exhibition. "That was bonkers!" Greta crows.

"I couldn't help myself." I take her hand in mine. "I needed an excuse—"

"An excuse for what?" she asks, taking another gulp of her violently pink beverage. She doesn't pull her hand away. Instead, she stares down at our entwined fingers, transfixed.

"To touch you."

♦ ♦ ♦

Greta moans as I kiss her neck, her fingers tangling in my hair. *More, more, more,* she urges without saying a word. I shuck her dress up her thighs, tearing at her stockings. When I led her out into the alley, she was anxious, casting her eyes left and right. But now, she is uninhibited, driven to desperation by my roving hands.

Suddenly, the bar's back door opens, a rectangle of light stretching into the dark. We freeze. A man strolls into the alley, lugging two bags of trash. He tosses them into a dumpster before heading back inside. He didn't notice us.

Greta giggles nervously. "Maybe we should go somewhere else," she whispers.

"Maybe," I reply, noncommittal. I press my lips against her neck, surreptitiously tasting her with the tip of my tongue. Heat pools in my groin at the very thought of sinking my teeth into her warm flesh. I've been dreaming about it for such a long time — dreams of ripping, chewing, and feeling satiated.

It'll be the sort of meal that makes you sigh in contentment, unbuttoning your fly to let your distended belly free. I am sure of it. It will surpass Thanksgiving dinner, or even the tastiest buck, its crown of antlers left in the dirt.

I can't wait much longer. While Greta's moaning under my hands, eyes half-lidded, I drag the flat of my tongue along her neck. She tastes like brine. I nibble her flesh with my flat teeth, making her whimper. My hard palate itches and saliva pools in my mouth, then trickles down my chin.

My jawbone unhinges, a sunspot bursting upon my somatosensory cortex. The bones of my face grate upon one another with a sickening *crunchhhh*, forming a muzzle and keen teeth. Strands of dark fur erupt from my pores, the sensation akin to a tickle. By the time a thick mane adorns my shoulders, my prey realizes something is wrong.

"Wha—" she manages, before I clap a large paw over her mouth. She mustn't scream. I don't want to have a quick bite—a snack just won't do. I've thought about this for a long, long time. Her breath is hot and quick against my leathery paw pads. I tower over her now.

She's such a small girl, isn't she? I could break her in half like a piece of kindling.

Finally, I take a bite. The taste is beyond anything I could have possibly imagined.

CHAPTER 2
(RAFE)

⊲◆⊳

The decommission of the USS *West Virginia* proceeds with little fanfare. Her turrets are dismantled, piece by piece. Anything worth saving is squirreled away in pockets and packs. Her crew departs, and no one bothers to look back. The hulking warship exemplifies everything we'd like to forget: the smoke burning our eyes and the stinky sweat clinging to our brows.

We don't speak to each other. There are no good-byes. We've shit in the same toilet for six months—there's nothing left to say.

I find myself lingering on the dock well after most of the sailors have joined their loved ones. It's strange to be ashore. I had become so accustomed to the rock and roll under my feet, the claustrophobia of the lower decks, the stink of unwashed bodies, and the rumbling of bombers overhead. Standing in the busy shipyard is akin to being tossed overboard into the cold, dark ocean: a shock so severe it can stop a heart.

There's a large part of me that wants to turn back, to climb back into the casemate below the turrets, where I'd spent most nights huddled with a shotgun. It was my job to protect the ammunition from saboteurs. I often felt like a mother dragon protecting her eggs. But now, those shells are being hoisted port side into another warship—the dreadnought *Pennsylvania*. Someone else will guard them now.

"Rafe!" Amidst the crowd, my brother Elton waves wildly. He's broad, built like a phalanx. The crowd gives him a wide berth to avoid getting bowled over. I shoulder my heavy duffel pack and trot to meet him, chuckling when he engulfs me in a tight bear hug.

"Nice to see you too," I exclaim, clapping him on the back. It's strange how someone can smell like home: stale cigarettes, Old Crow bourbon, and the Pine-Sol we use at the motel. "It's been a long time," I add when he finally releases me.

Suddenly, tears prickle my eyes, and I scrub them away with my forearm. I hadn't realized I missed my family this much. In the Pacific Theater, emotions were casualties of war.

Elton insists on taking my duffel. "The pickup is in the lot," he says, leading the way. "We can stop and grab something to eat on the way, if you'd like."

When we approach the truck, I hesitate, fingering the door handle. I can't bear the thought of getting inside. I've only just started to lose my sea legs.

"We can meet up in South Norfolk," Elton suggests. *He knows me so well*. "Go for a run. I'll follow you."

So, I run.

The ground is a rush beneath my paws. I scrabble over rocks and duck under tree branches, my ears pinned against my skull. It's been ages since I've been wolfish, and my whole body hums. *This is what it must feel like to be born:* being knotted like a fist and stretching for the first time, eyes blinded by a brilliant, white light.

Elton's truck chugs abreast for a mile or so, before quickly hitting traffic. I leave him behind; he'll catch up when he can.

The route isn't particularly pastoral, and the sun is high. I use the industrial buildings and warehouses as cover when the trees begin to thin out. I finally skid to a stop near the waterworks, panting. The building thrums with electricity, and it makes my hair stand on end.

A deer, grazing under the shadow of an auxiliary building, spots me. She raises her angular head, her fan-shaped ears prick forward. I have subsisted off of C-rations for months, and the thought of eating fresh meat makes me almost queasy with want. The doe eyes me, lock-kneed; she hopes I'll lose interest. We stare at one another.

With a powerful thrust of my haunches, I break into a sprint. The animal leaps and twists in midair, tripping over her own spindly limbs when she lands. I sink my teeth into her side, dragging her down. With a high-pitched bleat, she kicks at me, one cloven hoof glancing off my hip. The pain is sharp, immediate, but my mouth is full of warm, gushing blood.

She tastes so, so—

"I'm dying," the ensign cries, blood trickling from the corner of his mouth. The smell of copper fills my nose, and I hate how it makes my stomach grumble. I press my palms against the tangle that was once his shoulder, but there's no staunching the flow. The bullet nicked an artery, and it arcs between my fingers, soaking my clothes, the deck.

God, just one taste. I just want one. Little. Taste.

—*good.* I only raise my head when I hear the crunch of tires on gravel and the cough of an engine. It's Elton's rust bucket Ford. I leave what remains of my kill in the grass and lumber over, licking gristle out of my teeth.

"Feel better?" he asks, casually draping his wrist on the steering wheel.

With a stifled moan, I step out of my pelt. The painful conversion from man to wolf is immense. I was so eager to run that I'd barely registered it. But now, I am privy to every knitted muscle, every broken bone. I grip the truck's bed so that I don't topple over, the metal cutting into my palms.

"There's more, if you're hungry," I add when my jaw clicks back into place.

"I stopped at McDonalds," Elton says, shaking a cup with Speedee, the burger-headed mascot, on the side. The ice tinkles merrily.

I open the door to retrieve the clothes I had folded neatly therein, slipping them on. Elton wordlessly passes me a handful of paper napkins, and I blot the blood off my mouth and hands.

"Are you ready to go home?" he asks as I pull back on my crackerjack uniform. I accidentally smear blood on the starched lapel.

I nod.

♦ ♦ ♦

We arrive in Wharton just after sundown. The sky is the color of a bruise, casting a violet shadow over Main Street. Elton drives slowly, letting bandeau-clad girls trot across the street. "I love summertime." He chuckles.

I've always seen Wharton as sleepy, laggard. But since I've been gone, some of the storefronts have changed. Neely's Flowers is now Hart's Drugstore, selling malts for fifteen cents on Sundays according to the signage. Even Seaside Books, the oldest institution in town, is sporting a new awning. Surely, if the town has changed so much, I have too.

I look down at my hands, corded with thick veins. My nails are thin, cracked, delineated by dark, vertical ridges—a symptom of severe vitamin deficiency. My palms are still flaked with the doe's blood despite my best efforts to wipe it away.

It's not the only blood on my hands. Saliva drips down the back of my throat, threatening to gag me. I swallow it down. *Don't think about it.*

There's a small crowd gathered outside the courthouse, candles cupped in their hands. "What's going on?" I ask, rolling down the window, letting the salt air whip my hair back.

"I was going to tell you—"

11

"Tell me *what*?" Something in his voice is troubling. It's as though he's been caught, like he's stepped into a trap and must now decide whether he should chew his leg off.

Without taking his eyes from the road, Elton continues, "A few people have gone missing this summer." Despite the humidity, a chill trickles down my neck. "It's been the big story in the *Tribune*," he adds.

As we drive by the vigil, I crane my neck to see flyers pinned onto a corkboard in the courtyard. Typically, people post help wanted ads, birth and death announcements, and calls for prayer. But now, it's entirely papered in vacation photos: happy people sunning themselves, roughhousing, applying sunscreen, sipping drinks, and eating enormous lobster tails. The word MISSING is scrawled on each one.

"How many?" I ask.

"A few," Elton replies, evasive, cranking the wheel to turn into the Cove Motel's parking lot. His face is bathed in shadow. But I can see his jaw moving; he's chewing the inside of his cheek. It's a bad habit, born of childhood anxiety. He feels guilty about something.

"Was it you?" I ask as he parks. Elton frees the key from the ignition and fiddles with it, refusing to look at me. "*Was it you?*" I repeat, gritting my teeth.

"You know me better than that, Rafe."

"Then why won't you talk to me?"

He doesn't respond. Instead, he looks out the driver's side window. A group of pedestrians walk past, laughing. I can hear bits and pieces of their conversation. They aren't sure where to eat tonight.

I slap my palm on the dashboard, making Elton jump. "Talk to me!" I exclaim.

Without a word, Elton slides out of the car, retrieving my duffel from the truck bed. He still avoids my eyes when I get out, slamming the door. As we approach the front office, he hesitates. "Look, Rafe—" He scrubs his hands through his chestnut-colored hair, mussing it. "It's been different without you here. I think someone in the pack might be responsible. I just don't know who."

"Well, your Alpha is back," I snarl, taking my pack from his hands.

It's heavy, weighed down with the detritus of my last six months. And wrapped up in the very bottom, the bullet that I had used to shoot the man on the aft deck. The man who cried in my lap afterward as his blood seeped into my shoes.

The very last man.

II. 1947

CHAPTER 3
(AMA)

---◁◆▷---

P ilgrim State is an imposing edifice, consisting of a stone facade, a coil of ivy, and arched doorways. Inside, it is as quiet as a church. I find myself staring at a statue of Mary just to the right of the atrium, her arms raised upward in supplication. I can't tell if she's laughing or crying.

"Right this way, Miss."

The nurse's squarish heels clunk on the linoleum, her starched, white pinafore swishing around her knees. She has a spirited walk, seemingly unaffected by the general malaise of Pilgrim State. Conversely, my gait is sluggish, shuffling; the air inside the asylum feels inordinately heavy.

My escort is blissfully unaware of my inner turmoil. I fear that if she were privy to it, I wouldn't be allowed to leave the hospital. I can't help but imagine a bite block wedged between my jaws and the smell of cooking meat as my brain sizzles. *Would smoke trickle out of my ears afterward?* For a moment, I contemplate telling her I've changed my mind. *Oh goodness, I've left the stove on at home. Perhaps, I should come back another time.*

As we leave the administrative area and enter the ward, the air becomes as thick as molasses. It's almost as though I can taste it. I press my lips together and wrinkle my nose.

The nurse ushers me into a large common room. It's a depressing tableaux. Most of the patients sit around the tube, watching—but not *really* watching—*Kukla, Fran, and Ollie,* a children's program. A man, horribly thin, edges around the room, his fingertips brushing against the painted concrete walls. When he passes by, I hear him whisper, "I'm comin' home, mama."

The room is dreadfully quiet and inordinately loud all at once. The volume on the television is low, the red-nosed puppet's squawking voice barely discernible. The conversations are hushed, as if we are all attending a funeral.

And aren't we? *Here lies the human condition, borne away by madness.*

But there are screams too.

"Fuck you!" a man shouts as an orderly swaddles him in a straitjacket. Another rocks on his haunches and keens, picking at his pockmarked cheeks with dirty fingernails.

The nurse gives me an encouraging smile.

Bernie is one of the television-watchers. He is dressed in striped pajamas, the buttons halfway undone. I can just see the mole on his sternum, the spot where I used to kiss. It would always make him laugh. "C'mon Ama," he'd groan, red-faced. "You're driving me crazy."

"Bernard," the nurse says, resting her palm on his shoulder. "You have a visitor."

As if underwater, Bernie slowly turns his head. When our eyes meet, it's like looking into a lacuna. There's no immediate spark of recognition, no warmth, no chilliness either.

"Hey, Bernie," I manage to say, despite my rapidly thickening tongue. "How are you doing?"

A thin line of drool trickles from his downturned lips.

The nurse dabs it away. "He's feeling a little under the weather because of the new medication. Right, Bernard?"

"Mhmm," Bernie replies.

"I'll just help Bernard to a table, so you can talk," the nurse continues brightly. She reaches for Bernie's arm, hauling him upright. Despite looking at though she weighs almost nothing, the nurse is deceptively strong. Bernie shuffles obediently beside her as she leads him to a table in the corner, a stack of board games at its center.

I wait for Bernie to be guided into a seat before I sit, too. "You have ten minutes, Miss Chilton," the nurse reminds me kindly.

Bernie isn't looking at me. He looks up and out the window, the sun streaming over his brow. For a brief moment, I can almost imagine we are on a picnic in Central Park, enjoying the fresh, springtime air. But the breeze ruffling my hair isn't a breeze at all, but a coughing, hot wheeze from the ancient ventilation system.

And Bernie isn't quite himself, either.

"Bernie?" I ask, tentative. He doesn't look at me. Instead, his eyes flutter closed, and he heaves a great, long sigh. I cough. "Can you hear me? Do you know who I am?"

"Be quiet," he finally whispers. "I can almost hear the birds." Sure enough, I hear the faintest tittering, just beyond the tempered glass. A pigeon alights on the windowsill, shaking out its wings, damp with morning dew.

I rest my hands in my lap. I've bitten my nails to the quick fretting about this visit, and I don't want him to see. A fresh dribble of spittle meanders down Bernie's chin. Reflexively, I reach toward him to wipe it away, but I stop myself, thinking better of it. My hand hangs in the air between us, neither coming nor going.

My nails do look *awful*.

"I wanted to visit...to see if—" My voice trails off, unsure. I press my lips together. "I wanted to see if you were alright." *I wanted to see if you remember.*

Bernie finally opens his eyes, appraising me. There are circular-shaped burns on his temples, the skin raised and inflamed. Dr. Freeman had assured me he had been comfortable, but how comfortable could he have possibly been?

"Ama?" Bernie rolls the word around in his mouth, as if tasting it. *Ahh-muhh.*

"Your 'best girl'," I prompt, using his favorite term of endearment.

"Right," he says. "That's right. I'm sorry, I—"

"It's okay," I interrupt, waving away his apology.

"—I forget a lot of things," he finishes, undeterred. "Names, dates, that sort of thing." Bernie reaches across the tabletop, touching my knuckles with his calloused fingertips. It's a gentle tap, as if testing to see if I'm corporeal.

"We're engaged," I whisper. "We were, anyway, before."

"Before?" he asks.

Before I told you what I am. "Before the war," I clarify. "You were overseas, remember?"

"That's why I'm here," Bernie muses, examining the tabletop as if the wood grain might help him divine what has happened to him. "They said I haven't been *myself.*" The first time, Bernard had admitted himself. After the electricity zapped away what frightened him, he was put into a taxicab and sent home. The police found him in the street, calling out for his Sergeant. He was certain he was in Carentan, fighting Jerry. But he was meandering down Seventh Avenue, slapping the hoods of idling vehicles, fluid trickling from his nose.

"No," I agree. "You haven't." I adjust my skirt over my knees, tucking one ankle behind the other. "Do you remember me at all, Bernie?"

He stares at my face with such ferocity I can't help but avert my eyes. "You met my mama once," he finally says. "Right?"

"She and I still have lunch, sometimes."

"Does she ever talk about me?" he asks.

"All the time," I assure him. For the first time, he smiles. It's a crooked smile, all teeth. I've felt the curve of that very smile against the soft flesh of my thigh. A pang of grief threatens to overtake me. I miss him. *Us*.

"We're getting married in the spring," he says, speaking slowly as though he's trying to recall a movie he hasn't seen in a decade.

"We were meant to," I reply slowly. "It's summertime now. You've been here for three months."

"Oh." He looks crestfallen. "I ruined it, didn't I?"

I reach across the table, taking both of his hands in mine. "Oh, darling, no. It's not your fault. Not in the slightest. It's *mine*."

"Because of what happened," he says in a flat, matter-of-fact voice.

"I—" I think better of it and clamp my lips shut. Part of me had hoped he would have forgotten. As much as I hated his parents for agreeing to shock therapy, I had hoped that those memories had been jailed inside a piece of dead grey matter.

"It was real, wasn't it?" he asks. "What I saw?"

"What did you see?" I ask, my stomach clenching in painful knots.

"The wolf," he replies, "in the kitchen."

"I don't know what you're talking about," I reply, marveling at the smoothness of my own voice.

I can't stop looking at the ring, turning the diamond this way and that, each facet catching the light. It doesn't feel real yet.

Bernie, amused, watches me, his chin resting on his palm. "Are you happy?" he asks.

"So happy," I murmur, meeting his eyes across the kitchen table. They are a deep ocher, the color

of freshly tilled soil. "*I've never been happier.*" *It's not entirely true, but it's true enough. I don't think he could ever understand the uninhibited joy of chasing a deer through the trees, the autumnal leaves crunching underneath my paw pads. It is a feeling akin to euphoria. Transcendence.*

I had almost told him what I was several times before: in line at the bank, after he took me to meet his parents, and when we had sex for the first time in the back of the Lincoln Continental we had borrowed from his father's garage. But I was frightened. I feared he would scream, attack me, or worse: flee.

But now—

Now, he's my fiancé. And he ships out to France in the morning. His Army surplus duffel sits by the front door, my photo tucked into the side pocket.

"*I think I would like to show you something,*" *I say slowly, rising and stepping toward him.*

"*Oh yeah?*" *He fiddles with the buttons on my dress, his grin lascivious.*

"*Not* that!" *I squeal, slapping at his hands.* "*Just promise me to keep an open mind.*" *My voice wobbles, betraying my nervousness.*

Bernie leans back in his chair, surveying me. "*Sure.*"

I hesitate. I can still turn back. *But I let out a shuddering breath. The skin on my chest tingles, and nearly pellucid fur erupts from my pores. I imagine I must look like a shimmering mirage, the fur spreading over my body in ripples. With a resounding snap, my jaw dislocates and I squeeze my eyes shut tight, the white hot pain radiating downward as the curvature of my spine elongates; the bones in my limbs snap, lengthen,*

then knit back together; the butterfly wings of my ileum stretch to accommodate my thickening femurs.

My dress tears, puddling at my feet.

Dimly, I hear Bernie shout and the chair topple over. I crack open my eyelids. My fiancé has retreated to the far corner of the kitchen, pulling open a drawer with such ferocity the whole lot falls to the ground. He grabs the barbecue fork near his foot, wielding it like a sword, the sharp tines pointing at my chest.

"Bernie," I say, my voice gravely. But it's unmistakingly my voice. I'm still here. Surely, he can see that. I catch a glimpse of my reflection in the convex surface of the teapot. My wolven form is lithe, long-limbed, maned with a tapered waist and snout. I realize speaking forces my lips away from my teeth, making it appear as though I'm snarling. "I know this is frightening," I manage. "I'm sorry."

"What...what are you?" Bernie presses his spine against the wall, as if hoping he will sink through it. But he doesn't run. He's a soldier, after all.

"It's me," I insist. "I'm still me."

"You're a monster. Like in that movie."

We saw The Wolf Man *at the Roxy. I remember the date well. He brought me gardenias, and we shared a small bag of popcorn. In the dark, our buttery fingers laced together, and he kissed me unabashedly. The movie continued on despite our lapsing attention:*

"You killed the wolf," Maria Ouspenskaya had said on-screen.

"Well, there's no crime in that, is there?" Lon Chaney Jr. replied.

"I'm not a monster," I insist. "Bernie, it's me. It's Ama." I step out of my fur, the sudden cold of the kitchen making me shiver. Naked, I reach for him, forgetting to be bashful. "See? It's me." My voice sounds inordinately high. My heart pounds.

"I'm dreaming," he breathes, still gripping the fork. "This is a dream."

"It's—"

"I'm going home," Bernie sputters, dropping the fork. The metallic clatter makes us jump. "I'm tired. That's what this is. A hallucination." His jaw is tight and he avoids my eyes. He rights his chair and retrieves his coat from its back. When he skirts around me, he gives me a wide berth. "I'll write," he promises, before he shuts the door behind him. The tears that trickle down my cheeks are hot.

He didn't kiss me goodbye.

It is a relief to leave the asylum. As soon as I step over the threshold, my lungs fill with cool, springtime air. Inside, I inhaled only staleness and the reek of unwashed bodies; only shallow breaths kept me from retching onto the tile floor. When I finally step out of the monolith's shadow, I feel brave enough to look back at my fiancé's prison: brick walls, heavy doors manned by barrel-chested orderlies, and tempered windows covered by steel bars.

"Goodbye, Bernie," I whisper, before sliding into the driver's seat of my Chevrolet. I glance into the backseat, taking inventory: two suitcases, a toiletries bag, and a hat box brimming with keepsakes. I turn the key in the ignition, the engine starting with a purr.

I try not to cry when I leave the lot and make my way toward the Southern State Parkway.

♦ ♦ ♦

Exhausted, I pull off Route 60 at a truck stop, parking between two large freightliners. I've been driving south for hours, unsure of my final destination. There have been rumors of packs taking refuge in small towns along the East Coast, but so far, I haven't seen hide nor hair. In truth, I'm not quite sure I'm even heading in the right direction. Surely there won't be signage. *Wolves Ahead: Keep Right!*

I stretch, listening to the engine click, click, click as it cools. I smell horrific. My dress is badly wrinkled, and my hair sticks to the back of my neck. I must look exactly how I feel: road-weary. The truck stop is quite small, consisting of only two gas pumps and a Metroliner diner.

The metallic capsule is nearly empty, save for a buxom woman behind the counter and two men sitting at opposite ends. I presume they are the truckers whose vehicles flank my Chevy. "Hey there, sweetheart," the woman behind the counter croons.

"Good evening," I reply politely, perching on a stool.

"Good morning, more like it," the woman says, sliding a menu across the countertop. "It's two o'clock." She has a tattoo of a sparrow on her forearm, and I try very hard not to stare.

It's strange how time passes on the road. Sometimes, the hours fly by like mile markers. In other instances, a second seems like an eternity and a mile feels like an unreachable goal. Now, suddenly privy to the time, my body feels heavy. I can't imagine driving much further tonight.

"Could I get a cup of coffee?" I ask.

The woman grunts and pours a cup, placing it in front of me. "Anything else?" she asks.

"Just the coffee, thank you," I take a sip, wincing. It's strong, far stronger than what I am accustomed to. But the caffeine makes my fingers and toes tingle, and the never ending road doesn't seem quite as daunting. I take another gulp and it goes down easier this time. "Can you tell me what the nearest town is?" I ask.

"Wharton." The woman rests her elbows on the counter, surveying me. "Are you looking for a place to rest, or a place to stay?"

"Both."

"You could do worse than Wharton." The woman shrugs. "Go to the Cove Motel. Tell 'em Mags sent you."

The Cove Motel is kitschy, its sign decorated with plastic shells and a mermaid with long, stringy hair. The squat building is shaped like a U, with a large pool taking up the majority of its courtyard.

I find the door labeled OFFICE easily enough, but there's no one inside. There's a distinct odor, though it isn't a bad one. It smells earthy, like groundwater and bushmeat. I tap the bell on the countertop (ding!), but no one appears. "Hello?" I call. "Is anyone here?" The window-mounted air conditioner spits out cold air, and, despite the sweat upon my skin, I shiver.

"Sorry, sorry!" A large, shirtless man appears in the doorway. He's wearing only trousers, one suspender dangling at his hip. His eyes are swollen with sleep. "I didn't expect anyone to check in this late." His chest is covered in thick, russet chest hair.

"It's quite alright," I reply. "Could I get a room, please?" I search his face, looking for some telltale sign. But I'm not entirely sure what to look for. I've been alone for so long.

"Sure thing," he says, handing me a ledger to sign. "It'll be three dollars per night. How long are you planning to stay?"

I'm not sure. Surely, Wharton at three o'clock isn't indicative of Wharton in daylight. Most of the buildings were dark, their facades obscured by shadow. I could smell the salt in the air, but, from the road, I couldn't see the ocean. I've always wanted to live near the water, but this doesn't seem like a hospitable place for my kind. I've always imagined cabins in the middle of nearly impenetrable forests. Or campsites wedged inside massive cave systems.

The man eyes me curiously. "That's alright, ma'am, just pay for a night or two, then we can discuss a longer stay once the sun's up."

"Thank you," I say, relieved. *You could do worse than Wharton,* the woman had said. What was her name? "Mags sent me."

"That's my wife Margaret." The man grins. "I'm Elton. Nice to meet you." He grasps my hand in his veritable paw, giving it a hardy shake.

I can't help but smile. He's kind, albeit oafish. "I'm Ama." I fumble in my purse for the cash to pay him, placing a mess of bills and coins on the countertop.

"You're in room six," Elton announces, retrieving a key. There's a tacky seashell-shaped tag attached, the number 6 written in a jaunty script. I thank him, and head back out into the heat to find my room. I pass an alcove—occupied by both an ice chest and nickel candy machine—and two rooms between the office and my room.

My room is just as cold as the office, if not more so; the air conditioner makes the heavy curtain ripple like a slow-moving wave. I sit on the edge of the bed, turning the key in my hands. My luggage sits at my feet, untouched. In truth, I'm not sure what to do with myself now. My only desire was to flee New York—my guilt.

I lay back on the hard mattress, throwing an arm over my eyes. The room feels as though it's spinning, tilted on its axis. "Fuck!" I whisper aloud, before clapping my hand over my mouth, smearing my lipstick. That's not the language of a civilized lady. But I'm not civilized, am I?

"Fuck," I repeat to no one.

Invigorated, I sit up, reaching for the ice bucket. *I may as well make this home, at least for tonight.* The breezeway is quiet, just as I had left it mere moments ago. The heat presses its wet hand against the back of my neck. Sweat prickles under my arms. I backtrack to the ice box, shoveling a heaping scoop into my bucket. I select a piece and press it against my skin, the chilly water trickling between my breasts.

I catch a glimpse of myself in the office window, and I can't help but laugh. I look feral: my dress is wrinkled, my face is oily, my lipstick is a streak across my cheek, and my hair is a nest of flyaways. It's a wonder Elton hadn't rejected my money and sent me away to sleep in my car!

Then, I see the Help Wanted sign tacked to the office window.

CHAPTER 4
(RAFE)

◁◆▷

I'm late.

I hustle down Main Street, edging around the tourists loitering on the sidewalk. It's still early in the season, but the war is over now. Finally having an excuse to spend their money with wild abandon, the summer set descended on Wharton like fleas to a dog. I walk with a cigarette dangling out of my mouth, smoke curling from my nostrils like a jaunty handlebar mustache.

Every step is its own special torment. I would much rather be in bed with my latest.

"Oh Rafe, please stay," Emily—or is it Emilia?— pouts as I pull on my short-sleeved button down. I try, in vain, to smooth out the deep-set wrinkles with my palms. I should have draped it over the chair instead of tossing it into a heap on the floor, but I hadn't been thinking clearly.

I pad, barefoot, into the bathroom, filling my palm with cool water to drink.

"I've got to get to work," I remind her, pulling my slacks up and cinching my belt. I sit on the edge of the bed to put on my loafers.

"Don't I get a kiss?" Emily-Emilia pouts. She sits up, the bedsheets pooling around her waist. Her breasts, made blotchy by my teeth, are bare, the pink nipples pert. She wraps an arm around my chest, kissing the spot just behind my ear. Her tongue snakes over my earlobe.

"Five more minutes," I relent. *"On your knees, sweetheart."*

Despite a year passing since the *West Virginia* docked, I can't seem to shake the memory of the ensign on the aft deck. No matter how much I drink or fuck, I still hear his gurgling cry. Emily-Emilia tried her very best, but he was still there, looking down at me from the ceiling. Even when I closed my eyes, my fist knotted in her hair, I could still hear his rattling exhale.

Like the street, the Cove Motel is teeming with guests, most of whom are in some state of undress. Men walk around in swim trunks, while women wear form-fitting swim suits, their swing skirts leaving very little to the imagination. Children dart between clumps of adults, shrieking, their hair damp and smelling strongly of chlorine. All of the deck chairs are occupied by either bodies or towels. In the pool, swimmers are nearly elbow-to-elbow.

I can almost hear the *ca-ching* of the cash drawer.

I find Flora in the front office, her auburn pin curls creating a fuzzy halo around her heart-shaped face. "Rafe, thank god," she exclaims, balancing the phone between her ear and shoulder. "We've been swamped. The girl is in your office. She's been waiting for fifteen minutes."

"Which girl?" I ask as I pour myself a cup of coffee, eyeing my closed office door.

"The potential housekeeper," Flora replies, rolling her eyes. "You're supposed to interview her. Or are you no longer the owner of this shithole?"

"Watch it." I laugh. "Maybe she'll get your job."

The Cove is a shithole, but it's a profitable one. It certainly isn't a tourist's first choice when booking a stay in Wharton. The motel is a relic of the 1920s, wherein less was more profitable. From the street, it's wholly unremarkable. Inside, it's even more mediocre. Each room is exiguous and sparsely decorated: one or two beds, a small, lumpy armchair, and a bathroom complete with sink and bathtub.

At least there's a roof, one guest mused when he checked out, *and no leaks!*

"No one wants this job," Flora deadpans. "She's been waiting for fifteen minutes."

"Don't flip your wig," I snort.

"And don't fall in love," Flora adds as I head toward my office, coffee in hand. "She's a cookie."

The woman sitting in my office straightens up when I enter. She's a cookie, alright: apple cheeks, pink-painted bow lips, and dark, wavy hair pinned up into victory rolls. She wears a mint-green dress with a white collar, the hemline riding up to her knees.

"Mr. Blanchard," she says, rising and offering her hand to shake. "I'm Ama Chilton. It's a pleasure to meet you."

I take her hand. It's soft and cool. "Nice to meet you, Mrs. Chilton. Call me Rafe."

"*Miss*," she corrects me. "Thank you so much for meeting with me." She sits, knees together and ankles crossed, her hands in her lap.

I sink down into the leather chair behind my desk, stubbing out my cigarette in the glass ashtray. Then, I take a gulp of my coffee. It's lukewarm. *What good is Flora?*

"What brings you to Wharton?" I ask. Through my office window, I can see the entire parking lot and a sliver of Main Street beyond. It's nearing noon, and cars creep in and out of the lot as guests check-in and -out.

"I needed a change of scenery," she replies, "and I've heard such positive things about the Southeast."

"Surely you didn't hear that from anyone who's lived here." I chuckle. "Flora says you're applying for the housekeeping position."

"Yes, sir," Ama replies. "I saw the 'help wanted' sign when I checked in. I'm hoping to earn some money so I can rent an apartment here in town."

"So, you're planning to stay, then?"

"I think so," she replies, biting her lip.

I find myself distracted by her scent. She is wearing Femme de Rochas, a plum and sandalwood blend that is particularly popular. But there's something else too. It's a faint musk, reminiscent of wild mushrooms and fresh rainfall. It's the smell of damp fur and ozone. Can she smell me, too? "So," I say casually, "you must not be frightened, then?"

"Frightened of?" she asks. Her hands in her lap clench; the knuckles blanch white. She wears her innocence like armor. I want to pick that facade away and reveal what is underneath. *Who are you?*

"There are rumors," I whisper, leaning forward conspiratorially. "Rumors of wolves prowling the woods outside of town."

Ama swallows. "Well, sir," she murmurs. "I'm not frightened of wolves."

"Brave girl," I remark, lighting another cigarette. "Do you have any experience?"

Ama's eyes widen in alarm. "Experience, sir?" She worries an errant strand of her hair with her fingers, knotting it. It's as though she can't quite sit still. She can't look at me either—not directly. Her eyes wander around the room and settle somewhere at my chest. Surely, she can hear my heart beating. I can hear hers. It's pounding like a bass drum.

"Housekeeping," I prompt. Her reaction is the proof in the pudding, so to speak.

"No, sir. But I'm a quick learner." I like how she says, *sir.* It's titillating.

I rise from my chair, meandering around the room while I think of how to proceed. To her credit, she stays silent, merely gazing at the spot where I once sat. I finally lean against my desk, crossing my arms. She leans away from me.

"You'll start first thing tomorrow," I announce. "But on a trial basis, of course."

"Of course," Ama parrots. She rises, and for a brief moment, we are eye to eye. Up close, her eyes are the blue of swelling waves. "Thank you for the opportunity," she says shyly, skirting around me and out the door.

Her scent lingers, even long after she's gone.

♦ ♦ ♦

The motel quiets in the early evening. Most of the guests retire to their rooms before dinner or stroll through town buying chotskies. Only the very dedicated sunbathers and beachcombers remain beachside; the setting sun and the ceaseless breeze makes it chilly. I push aside the administrivia I've been working on and toss my pen on top, eager to head to The Dock. It's my usual haunt: dark and quiet, with drinks that aren't watered down.

Flora is still in the office proper, her chin resting in her palm, her eyes half-lidded. "Asleep on the job?" I ask, startling her.

"There hasn't been anyone in here for over an hour," she moans," and Samuel is late."

"Sam is always late." I rest my forearms on the countertop and sigh. Outside, I catch a brief glimpse of Ama striding into the alcove with her ice bucket dangling from her fingers.

"He can sure hold a grudge," Flora adds, giving me a sidelong look.

"He can sure be a problem," I correct her.

The pack is waiting in the office for me, helium balloons bobbing near the ceiling. "Welcome home!" Nico crows, grasping my upper arms and shaking me excitedly.

Sorry, *Elton mouths, unceremoniously dropping my duffel beside the front desk. He looks as though I* slapped him. I may as well have. I very rarely flaunt my position as Alpha, especially when it comes to my sibling. It's a sore spot between us, one I have little desire to pick at.

I shrug Nico off, surveying the tow-headed boy in his too-large clothes. I can't help but imagine blood dripping off his chin. Which of the missing people is he responsible for, if any? Samuel—his dark hair slicked back and oily—gives me a tight smile. Flora and Mags bound to embrace me, the latter kissing each of my cheeks.

"Who's going to answer for it?" I ask when the fanfare ebbs. My jaw clenches tight, my teeth scraping together with a high-pitched squeal. I don't want to celebrate. I want answers.

"He knows," Elton elaborates. The images of happy people living their last days plague me. I think of their loved ones, lighting candles, hoping for guidance in the darkness. I think of how the dark, rolling ocean swallowed up the ensign after I pushed his body overboard.

Samuel shrugs. "What do we have to answer for?"

"We don't hunt humans, and we don't hunt at home," I snap, stepping toward the taller man. The others reflexively step back.

"Who said we did?" Samuel asks. "That's a pretty huge accusation, Rafe."

I laugh; it's a short, barking sound. "We are all— any one of us—capable." I certainly was. Aboard the U.S.S. West Virginia, the castemate beneath the turret was boiling hot, and I had to wipe the sweat from my eyes before aiming at the vulturous Zeros circling overhead. Wipe, aim, fire. Their engines were *a high-pitched whine, and I only knew my aim was true when the sound ceased. I killed hundreds of pilots thusly.*

Nico looks pained. "Rafe—" But after a withering look from Samuel, the younger man falls silent.

"This is my pack," I snarl, making eye contact with each of them. Most have the sense to look chagrined. But Samuel is defiant, his jaw set, and his brow furrowed.

"Maybe it shouldn't be," he whispers. "If you are going to accuse us of something so foul."

If we weren't in the office, I would grasp him by the scruff of the neck and shake him hard, a warning. Instead, I jab my finger into the center of his chest. "Don't challenge me," I snarl. My whole body shakes with kinetic energy; anger courses through every nerve ending. "Unless you want a challenge."

"I'm not," he replies coldly.

"Sure," I scoff. "Now, I want you all to listen. If anyone so much as touches a human, I will kill you myself. We eat deer, rabbits, or you go to fucking McDonalds."

Samuel, still angry, avoids my eyes. But the others nod. Flora looks pale, a little sick. Elton wraps an arm around Mags' shoulders.

"'Welcome home,'" I scoff, heading into my office and slamming the door.

CHAPTER 5
(AMA)

ousekeeping is mindless. I spread fresh linen on beds, tucking them under the mattress. I tidy the countertops in the bathroom, sweeping stray hairs into a moist towel, then tossing it into my rolling bin to wash later. I like to open the windows before I start cleaning a room, so I can smell the sea breeze.

Room Sixteen is my favorite. From that window, I can see just a sliver of the beach and the rolling waves beyond it. I take my time cleaning, lingering in front of the window with a bottle of neon-blue Windex and a bit of newspaper. I wipe the glass in wide, sweeping circles, tracing the flight patterns of seagulls across the sky.

"Hey." Flora floats in and flops belly-first onto the bed. She looks stylish in a long-sleeved blouse tucked into a pair of high-waisted linen slacks. "How's your first week going?" she asks.

"Very good, thank you," I reply kindly. Flora is a carefree soul, seemingly unencumbered by feminine norms. I've often seen her in the front office, her feet propped on the countertop, smacking a thick wad of gum in her brightly painted mouth. I find it enviable.

"Have you met anyone else? The guys, I mean." She shifts so she can reach into her pocket, producing a compact. In it, she checks her makeup, licking the pad of her thumb to rub off a bit of her lipstick that had smeared.

"Just Mr. Blanchard and Elton." I've only seen the others: a surly-looking man with a penchant for spear-point-collared shirts named Samuel, and a baby-faced, ungainly teenager who dresses as though he lives in the tropics. I've never seen the latter in the same Hawaiian print twice.

"Rafe is making you call him 'Mr. Blanchard'? Gross." She wrinkles her freckled nose.

"No," I correct her. "But he's my boss." I haven't exchanged words with Rafe either, not since my interview. In truth, I've hardly seen him. And when I have, it's like he can divine my innermost secrets from just one look. *There are rumors of wolves prowling the woods outside of town*, he'd said.

"Well," Flora says, shutting her compact with a snap, "don't let him intimidate you. He's all bark and no bite."

"He *is* intimidating," I admit, picking up a pillow from the bed, then fluffing it in my hands.

"He's just broody." Flora chuckles. "He's had a rough few years. He was in Japan, you know."

"I didn't," I reply.

Intrigued, I forget my task and sit on the bed beside the reclining woman. I squeeze the pillow in my hands, desperately wanting to know *more*. But I'm not entirely sure why. Part of it is simple curiosity. But is it that entirely? Rafe is objectively handsome, isn't he? I hate to admit it, but I can't help but think about that moment in his office, when we stood so, *so* close together.

Seemingly eager to gossip, Flora sits up. "He served six months on a dirty, smelly warship a year ago. He rarely talks about it, but he came home in a *horrific* mood."

I can't help but to think of Bernie, slouched in the Pilgrim State common room. He looked like an abandoned marionette, its strings loose and its body sagging. "That's awful," I murmur.

"But," Flora amends, "Rafe really is a kind man, underneath everything. You just have to dig for it." She abruptly pops up off the bed. "I've got to get back to the desk. Maybe we could get a drink sometime. It's nice to have another girl around. Mags is always so busy with her kids."

"Sure," I say brightly.

After she leaves, I find myself tethered to the spot. I've tried very hard not to think about Bernie. But now, the thoughts come unabated. I can't help but to think of what our life would have been like at this very moment, if I hadn't told him my secret. Surely, we would have purchased a little saltbox home on the Hudson. I had always dreamed of living near the water. We would have married, maybe tried to have a child—or children. But we never had a chance to dream about our future family, coiled together in our marriage bed. *I ruined it*.

As if sleepwalking, I reach for the telephone on the bedside table. I turn the rotary dial, while inwardly screaming. *No, no, don't do that!* The phone rings, clicks, then there's a familiar voice on the line: "Hello?" *It's Bernie's mother, Louise.*

"Mrs. Edwards, it's Ama," I say before I lose my nerve. I want to slam the phone into the cradle, but I also can't bring myself to do it. I want to hear how Bernie is. Has he noticed I'm gone? I think of his vacant eyes.

"Ama! Darling! Bernie told us you'd visited!" *He remembers.* My heart feels as though it is in a vice grip. I'm finding it hard to breathe. I press my hand against my sternum, ensuring my heart is still beating. It hammers against my palm.

"I'm out of town," I say in a rush. "But I wanted to check in on Bernie."

"Oh, where are you staying, dear?" Louise asks. I can hear the familiar sounds of the Edwards household in the background: the dog barking, the jangle of his collar, the sound of running water as Louise washes dishes. I imagine her elbow-deep in suds, the phone tucked against her shoulder, her hair probably still in curlers.

"It's just a little town called Wharton," I reply, hoping I don't sound as impatient as I feel. I don't want to talk about myself.

"Bernie is feeling so much better, darling," Louise says. "He's home. Let me get him for you." I hear the water shut off and the shuffle of her feet on the tile floor. The phone line crackles. "Bernard!" she calls, her voice distant.

He's home? He's home! In my haste to hang up, I drop the phone on the floor. I haul it up by the coiled cord, nearly launching it into the air.

"Hello, Ama, *hello*?" a familiar male timbre says.

I hurriedly replace the receiver in the cradle and groan. *Stupid*. And yet…it's apparent he wanted to speak to me, too. Or, I amend, maybe he wanted to properly chastise me for abandoning him, for breaking his brain, for all of it. I lay back on the mattress, my skirt fanning on the bedspread. I press the heels of my hands into my eye sockets and groan.

I push the trash bin down the breezeway, trying very hard not to inhale the smell of rotting garbage. I park it near the dumpster, but don't finish my task. There's a light on in Room Twelve, and the door is cracked. *Did a guest forget to lock their door before going out for the evening?* I stride toward the door, intending to simply close it, but then, I catch a glimpse of who is inside.

Rafe Blanchard lays prone on the bed. His hand, dangling off of the side, grips a silver flask, the top unscrewed. It is in danger of spilling on the carpet. The carpet *I* had just vacuumed an hour ago. I stand in the doorway for a moment, looking for signs of life. He's breathing, but his eyes are closed. He certainly doesn't acknowledge my presence, nor does he seem to know I'm there. He must be asleep. I creep into the room, gently taking the flask from his hand and replacing the lid before placing it on the bedside table.

Task complete, I turn to leave the room. I'll lock the door and Rafe can sleep it off. But, before I can move more than two steps, his once-dangling hand encircles my wrist. "What are you doing?" he slurs.

Startled, I shriek, jerking my hand out of his grasp.

"Oh god," Rafe groans, placing his hands over his ears. "Don't be so loud, my head is killing me."

"Do you often make it a habit of sleeping in guest rooms?" I ask, looking down at him. He's somewhat sweaty and pale. He licks at his dry lips with his flat, pink tongue. He certainly doesn't look handsome now. Pathetic, really.

"Only sometimes," Rafe grumbles. He sits up, running a hand through his disheveled hair. Despite his best efforts, it still stands on end. He looks like a harried lion. "What are you doing here?"

"The door was unlocked."

"Help me up, will you?" He holds out his hand, and I take it.

It's clammy, and my fingers slip through his. With my other hand, I grasp his wrist, using both hands to yank him to his feet. He grasps my shoulder for support, his thumb pressing firmly against my clavicle. It's a strangely intimate gesture, and I gasp. I am struck, then, by his smell. It reminds me of decaying leaves on the forest floor: faintly cloying, yet not altogether unpleasant.

Before I can even process it, he's on the move again.

"I'm going home," he says. "Thank you for your help, doll." He grabs his flask and heads toward the door, somewhat meandering. He turns back to face me when he reaches the doorway. "I know your secret, you know," he adds, grinning like a Cheshire cat.

My stomach clenches. "My secret?" My voice sounds too high, too stilted.

He nods, sagely, but doesn't elaborate. "Goodnight, Ama." He chuckles, before heading toward the parking lot.

I watch him go. There's no way he knows. He can't possibly have any inkling. Except, he'd said it himself: *"There are rumors of wolves prowling the woods outside of town..."*

CHAPTER 6
(RAFE)

⊲◆▷

I can't get the blood out. I stand in the cramped head of the warship, scrubbing my clothes in the sink. Never mind that there's never a sink in the head—no room for one.

Someone knocks on the door. "Hey! I have to take a shit!"

"One minute!" I shout, never taking my eyes off my task. While the water turns pink, the stains seem to spread across the fabric. Suddenly, I'm not holding my clothes at all. Instead, I hold a large blood clot under the stream, willing it to dissipate.

"Open the door! Open the door! Openthedoor!"

"One minute!" I sob. I look up into the mirror, finding that I'm drenched in blood. It drips down my cheeks, as thick as mud. How will I clean all of this up? Just before the blood seeps into my eyes, I catch a glimpse of the ensign standing behind me, his maw open in a silent scream. His mouth is an abyss.

I wake up with bleary eyes and a dry mouth. The ensign that had been darting around my periphery—whispering curses into my ears—dissipates like all nightmares do. By the time I rise, stumbling into the kitchen, I barely remember his nighttime visit. Still, he's left a stain on me. While I wait for my drip coffee to brew, I wipe the sleep from my eyes.

I only have vague memories of last night, of wandering into Room Twelve and deciding to lay down to stop the room from spinning. I remember Ama's thin wrist in my grip, her skin cool. Then, I remember vomiting in my bathroom when I finally arrived home.

I'm not sure what I said to the housekeeper, but her eyes are emblazoned in my memory: a bright blue, and, when viewed up close, a tiny thread of gold.

When my coffee is finally done, I take a prolonged sip. It's scalding, and I cough around the immediate pain. *Fuck.* I carry the mug into the bathroom, turning on the water. *I'm going to be late, but I can't forgo a shower.* I still smell like vomit, and a veritable distillery leaks out of my pores.

When I step under the hot stream, I sigh. It's refreshing. I scrub my skin with a Camay soap bar until I am bright pink. Perhaps I can scrub the previous night off of me. I imagine it swirling down the drain.

Like blood.

I find myself thinking of Ama, looking down at me. Her face pinched, her disapproval lining her skin. She stood with her hip cocked out, her hand resting on its curve. Everything about her body language screamed *I'm disappointed in you.* I wonder what Ama would have done if I had pulled her down onto the bed with me. Maybe I could have unbuttoned her dress, smoothing the wrinkles out of her flesh with my tongue.

◆ ◆ ◆

I am still in a discordant mood when I walk into the front office. Nico is manning the desk, and a guest is waxing poetic about the luxuries provided at the Wharton Great Inn. "They have a diner," the man extolls, "with half-priced breakfast for guests. It was only fifty cents! But here? There's just an old candy machine that stole my nickel."

"I'm sorry, sir—" Nico manages before the man continues.

"They also let you swim in the pool after eight o'clock. I don't understand why your pool is closed earlier. I think that—"

I sigh loudly and theatrically, drawing both mens' attention. "Golly, mister," I say. "It sure sounds like you would have a *much* better time at the Great Inn. Fifty cents for a piece of toast and a scoop of runny eggs sounds just *lovely*."

The guest's face reddens. "I think that," he huffs. "I would like to speak to the manager."

"You're speaking to the owner." I chuckle, stepping through the partition separating guests from employees. "Nico, refund this man his money for the rest of his stay. He can pay double at the Inn."

The man sputters as Nico obediently opens the till. "That's not what—" the man whines, but I raise my hand to silence him.

The Beast Within Me

"Customer service is our priority, sir. Now, you have a *great* rest of your vacation." With a final wave, I head into my office, shutting the door firmly.

Moments later, Nico knocks and pokes his head in. "Thanks, boss. He was going on for a while."

"Show some moxie next time," I reply coolly, pointing my finger at him. "What would you have done if I hadn't shown up? Taken a beating?"

Nico frowns, dejected. "I didn't want to lose a guest. You would have chewed me out if—"

"—and now I'm chewing you out for the inverse," I snap. I shouldn't be scolding the boy; he's young, and it's not his fault I'm hungover. "Look." I sigh. "Just... go back out front and mind the register."

The younger man nods, and shuts the door. I press the heels of my hands into my eyes until starbursts explode. This is going to be a long, *fucking* day. *Will anyone notice if I crawl underneath my desk and take a nap?*

After an hour of opening envelopes and making note of bills needing to be paid, I rise, stretching until it feels like every vertebrae pops back into place. I have a bad habit of sitting hunched over, folded into myself.

My office is stuffy, and I long to breathe fresh air and enjoy the outdoors. Thankfully, I do have an excuse. I need to check on the candy machine, which supposedly swallows nickels without burping up gumballs. I open the bottom drawer of my desk, searching for a screwdriver. I keep odds and ends herein: stubs from movies: my dog tags (Blanchard, Rafe, H. 27748399 NP TYPE-AB- T. 10/45 USN); and various tools, screws, nails, and fastenings. I select a screwdriver.

46

It's mid-morning, and the breezeway is blissfully quiet. Most of the guests are still sleeping off their own hangovers or have already staked their claim on the beach. In summertime, one must set up umbrellas and beach chairs early, to avoid either an obstructed view of the waves or having to sit too close to a sun-reddened stranger.

I slot a nickel into the candy machine, turning the crank. Sure enough, nothing comes out. I unscrew the side panel, examining the inner workings of the machine. I poke my finger into the dispenser, looking for a clog. Then—*there!*—two gumballs wedged tight. I stick the head of the screwdriver into the chute, jabbing.

Oomph! Something hard strikes me in the back, pushing me against the machine.

"Oh god," a familiar voice squeaks. "I am *so* sorry, Mr. Blanchard!"

It's Ama, pushing her housekeeping cart. "What the *fuck* are you doing?" I snap, nearly throwing the cart aside.

"I'm sorry—"

"What if I had been a guest? Watch where you're going, girl." Her lower lip trembles, and she blinks rapidly. "I'm tired of having to babysit the lot of you today." She whispers something incomprehensible. "What the fuck did you say?" I snarl.

"I said: 'don't speak to me like that, sir.'" Ama grips her cart with white knuckles, her nostrils flaring in agitation. Despite the fat tears brimming in her eyes, she puffs her cheeks. "I don't deserve to be cursed at."

I step around the cart, until we are eye to eye. This close, her smell fills my nostrils. She's been using the miniature Ivory soaps we provide guests, heavily perfumed. But I can smell her wolfishness beneath: the odor of the air before rain, the sweetness of wild-flowers. Surely, she can smell me, too. Why hasn't she ever said anything?

Ama steps back, her back pressing against the humming ice machine.

"I'm becoming very tired of this game," I mutter.

"Sir?" her voice wobbles.

I rest my palms against the ice machine, bracketing each side of her head, effectively trapping her. I lean close. "How did you know?"

"How did I know what?"

"Stop playing dumb, Ama." Suddenly, Ama's palms slam into my chest, pushing me back. She's strong—much stronger than I could have surmised—and I stumble. We stare mutely at one another for a brief moment, our breath nearly synchronous.

She bares her teeth at me, which looks absurd with her human facade. "Don't talk to me like that," she snarls. Tears roll down her cheeks, but her voice is even, preternaturally calm.

In a single stride, I've pressed her back against the wall again. We are so close our breath comingles, hot and fast, so close I could practically kiss her. The thought of it makes my groin clench. *Can she can feel my desire rolling off me in waves? God.* "If you're staying in Wharton," I say, licking my lips, "you have to run with us."

"I don't know what you're talking about," she replies, insolent.

"Stop." I can't help myself. I stroke the very edge of her jaw with the pad of my thumb. "Run with us, wolf girl."

♦ ♦ ♦

I find Flora already at our usual meeting spot, sitting back on her haunches. Her reddish fur looks cocoa-colored in the twilight. "Rafe," she says by way of greeting. Her cloying falsetto sounds otherworldly through wolfish lips and teeth.

"Where are the others?" I ask. It rained earlier in the evening, and the ground is still wet and cool beneath my paws.

"Late," she replies, raising her shoulders in a shrug. "As usual. I hope they get here soon. I'm starving."

I catch a whiff of her before I see her. Ama clambers up the rise toward the water tower, huffing and puffing. She's still in human form, and the hemline of her dress is caked in mud.

"Oh," she exclaims when she spots us. "I'm sorry, I wasn't sure whether I should be—" Her hat falls off into a mud puddle and she sighs. I snort, my nostrils flaring. "Just give me a minute," Ama snaps. I am four times larger than her, and she seems entirely unaffected by it. "I'm Ama," she says to Flora.

"We've met," Flora replies.

"Oh?" Ama unbuttons her dress, revealing a silken bra, panties, garter belt, and stockings. I try very hard not to seem like I'm staring. But every inch of milky skin draws my eyes like a moth to a flame.

"'Welcome to Cove Motel, how can I help you'?" Flora says, artificial hospitality dripping from every tooth.

"Oh yes!" Clad in just her peachy-pink underwear, Ama folds up her dress and drapes it over one of the water tower's horizontal support beams. "Nice to see you, Flora." She reaches behind her, her shoulder blades nearly touching as she contorts to unclasp her bra.

I catch only a brief glimpse of her breasts before she modestly covers herself with her forearm.

"You're staring," Flora stage-whispers at me.

Ama looks over her shoulder at me, tilting her head. "Could you turn around, please?" she asks.

"Fine," I grumble, turning my back.

I listen as Ama removes the remainder of her clothes and folds them neatly into a pile at her feet. Then, the telltale snap of bone makes me forget my accordance, and I turn back just in time to see her fall forward, her palms pressing against the wet earth. Her tail sprouts from the spot just above her buttocks, while fur covers each of her haunches. It's white, as pure as freshly fallen snow.

When she raises her head, she looks at me with large almond-shaped eyes, their depths oceanic. Before she can say a word, our attention is diverted. Three wolves crest the hill: Mags, a mottled grey; Nico, silvery with a caramel-colored snout; and Elton, charcoal-colored. "Where's Sam?" I ask.

"Not coming," Mags replies, her normal deep voice sounding downright grating. "He's watching the motel."

The six of us head into the forest. As we walk, the trees grow closer together, their branches interwoven into complicated patterns. The moonlight barely penetrates the foliage, so we must step carefully. For a while, the only sound is our footfalls, until Ama whines. We all pause, our ears tipping forward. Sure enough, I hear what she had: a branch snapping, then the sound of scraping.

I can smell him before I see him. Then, *there!*

A large buck shoulders aside a low-hanging branch, scraping his enormous rack against the bark. He's marking his territory. The animal is huge. With his antlers, he is as tall as I am, and he is corded with thick muscle. I certainly wouldn't take him on alone. But there are six of us.

I wait for him to dip his head, snagging a bite of persimmon. Then, I lunge toward him. The others are fast behind, and we spread out in an attempt to corner him. The buck jerks his head up, spots us, then gallops back the way he came. He's fast, and I fear he will outrun us; he knows the forest better than we do. But then, a white streak courses past me. It's Ama, low to the ground, her footfalls sure. With a leap, she nearly lands on the buck's back, knocking him to the earth.

The buck throws his head back, and she yelps. He caught her just beneath the eye with one of the sharp points, and blood trickles down her cheek. Taking advantage of her lapsing attention, the deer escapes from beneath her, scrabbling to regain his feet. His

51

front leg snapped in the fall, and he grunts in surprise. He falls heavily to his knees.

Catching up, I grasp his throat between my teeth, careful to avoid his swinging horns. Seconds later, Mags is at his shoulder, sinking her teeth into the meat there. I snap his neck with a twist. I don't want him to suffer.

While the others eat, Ama steps away. Her muzzle is soaked in blood, and it drips off her chin. I step over the buck's body, approaching her. "Are you okay?" I ask.

Her fur melts, seeping back into her pores. As her skull shifts, she moans, raising her paws to her face. When her femur shortens, she loses her balance, falling onto her butt. Naked, she pulls her knees to her chest, her hands hiding her face. Blood trickles through her fingers.

The ensign's blood spurts, and I can't hold it in. I reach into the wreckage, searching for the artery. It slips through my fingers, and—

No, I scold myself. *Don't think about that!*

"Let me see," I prompt, kneeling beside her. I touch her shoulder with my oversized paw.

Ama slowly takes her hands away. The deer's antler scraped the ridge of her cheekbone, drawing a ragged line from her ear to her nostril. It's bleeding profusely, but it is only a superficial wound. "I'm dizzy," she moans.

"Let me take you home," I say gently. "Hop on." She looks up at me, not comprehending. "You can't transform again, not right now." It will irritate the wound, possibly causing the skin to tear further.

She rises, trying to cover her nakedness with her hands. I crouch, waiting for her to swing her leg over, her heels gripping my sides. Her fingers tangle in my scruff. "I'm ready," she whispers. She's not too terribly heavy, and I can carry her easily.

"Hold on tight," I tell her, setting off. I trot through the trees, heading back toward town. Eventually, she rests her cheek on my fur, her hands encircling my neck. I desperately want to take care of her.

I take the beachfront route to the motel, knowing there won't be people out there this late. When I can see the building on the horizon, most of its lights extinguished, I kneel so Ama can slide off. She looks far worse than she did in the forest. The blood is beginning to clot, and her skin is shiny with swelling. I shake off my wolfishness, fisting the sand and gritting my teeth to avoid crying out.

We must be a sight: two naked people standing amidst the dunes, both pale and shaking.

I take her hand, leading her toward the motel. "Come on, let's hurry." She has to trot to keep up with my long strides, but she doesn't complain. Under the shadow of the Cove Motel, we skirt around the building. I peer into the breezeway. Thankfully, it's vacant.

"Let's go to the office," I whisper. "Quickly now." We dart down the breezeway, the concrete cool under our feet, and into the office.

Samuel, manning the desk, looks up at us curiously. "What happened?" His eyes unabashedly sweep up and down Ama's naked form. The corner of his lip twitches. I reach beneath the desk for the Carlisle Kit, finding the small tin by touch alone. Then, I snag a clean towel from the pile we keep for guests.

"Just watch the desk," I snap, putting an arm around Ama's shoulders and steering her into my office.

Once inside, I retrieve one of my suit jackets and drape it over her shoulders. She pulls the fabric close. Her pale lips tremble.

"Let me clean you up," I say gently. From my glass-topped minibar, I grab a bottle of whiskey. "This won't be pleasant," I continue, "so take a nip of this." She nods, and I tip some into her waiting mouth.

"I'm ready," she whispers.

I open the kit, complete with gauze bandage and sulfanilamide. Then, I gently swipe the blood away with the towel.

Ama winces. "Gentle," she reminds me. "It hurts."

I press the bottle of whiskey into her hands. "You need to have a stiff upper lip," I say. "That's what they used to tell us in the military, anyway." When I reach for the antibacterial powder, she takes a large swig from the whiskey bottle, the amber liquid sloshing.

"That doesn't sound helpful," she snorts.

"It wasn't," I agree, tilting her chin up so I can tip some of the powder onto her cheek. "Don't move."

"I think my fiancé would have been happier if he hadn't been told that," she muses.

"Fiancé?" My hand stills. She has never mentioned anything about her life before Wharton. It's as though she just materialized here, shiny and new.

"Former," she clarifies, meeting my eyes. "He was stationed in France. I made a mess of it."

I unwrap the gauze bandage, applying it to her wound with gentle fingers. We are so close, stark naked, my hands caressing her face. *God. I want to kiss her.*

But Ama averts her eyes, and the spell is broken.

"You know," she murmurs, "that was the first time I've ever been with a pack."

I'm not altogether surprised. She wouldn't have been injured if she had stayed with the group, rather than running ahead. I can't imagine not having a pack—a de facto family. "Surely, you've had somebody," I say.

"Never," she insists. "My father was my only touchstone, but he was never around. He was a souse. I think...he really hated what he was."

"That's too bad." I reach for the pack of cigarettes on my desk and offer her one. She nods, mutely. I put both in my mouth, lighting them and puffing until they catch. Then, I hand her one. She holds it limply in her hand, watching the smoke coil toward the ceiling. "How are you feeling?" I ask.

Ama takes a drag, smoke seeping from the corners of her mouth. "It hurts. Thank you for helping me." She crosses her long, slender legs. "I'm sure you would have rather feasted on that buck instead."

"Nonsense," I soothe. "It's fine." A strand of her hair is stuck to the adhesive, and without thinking, I free it. My knuckles brush against her skin, and she trembles. I want to wrap my arms around her and tell her she's home. I can't imagine exploring wolfishness by oneself. How did she become such a fearless hunter?

"I should probably go to my room," Ama says. "I need to get cleaned up. Besides, I have an early shift tomorrow."

"Your boss sounds like a real asshole," I snicker. "Maybe you should hit him with another cart."

CHAPTER 7
(AMA)

⊲◆⊳

It is strange to walk through Wharton with a bandaged face. Most people stare openly at me, until I catch their eye. Then, they walk hurriedly away, as if I am contagious.

I stop at Hart's Drugstore for a malt, taking a sip of it at the counter. It's my day off, and my first time truly exploring Wharton proper. After licking cocoa off my lips, I continue onward.

I pass several shops, peering in the windows. I idle outside of Seaside Books, perusing the bestsellers: *For Whom the Bell Tolls, Native Son, The Heart is a Lonely Hunter, Nineteen Eighty-Four.* Then, I step inside a women's boutique, admiring a gorgeous satin blouse with butterfly sleeves and a matching clutch—embroidered with delicate appliqués—and inspect a rack of Clair McCardell dresses.

With the sun high in the sky, I take the short walk to the beach. I pass the courthouse and pause, the fluttering of paper catching my eye. There's a large bulletin board there, photos papering every conceivable surface. The photos overlap, as if vying for attention. There's a photo of a woman doing a headstand in the sand, her feet kicked skyward. Someone scrawled GRETA THORPE, MISSING SINCE 6/19/47 across the top. Another photo of a shirtless man holding a shell to his ear says GERRY CALLHOON, MISSING SINCE 7/7/47.

There are others too, the names and dates running together into one horrifying headline: 5 people went missing near Wharton Beach in the summer of '47. "God save us all" someone had graffitied. Despite the humidity, a chill trickles down my spine.

I can't stop thinking about the photos as I slip off my heels, walking barefoot in the sand. It's hot on the soles of my feet, and I dance from foot to foot. I race to the shoreline, splashing into the tide until the swell soaks my hemline. The water is cold, and gooseflesh travels up my pale legs.

I'm not quite dressed for it, but I sit in the sand anyway. I cross my legs, knee over knee, and lean back on my palms. The sea air ruffles my hair, and I inhale deeply. Despite the incessant throbbing in my cheek, I am content. The hunt last night was invigorating, and despite the outcome, it was nice to run with other wolves.

I've never had that kind of support before.

Drake Chilton is an imposing man. Even sitting in his wheelchair, he gives one the impression of loftiness, of being looked down upon. He's always been somewhat austere, but since my mother died, he's become inflexible. Especially when it comes to me.

When I come home with brambles in my hair and dirt streaking my cheeks, he is stern. I've done what is expressly forbidden. "Ama Marie Chilton," he says, enunciating every syllable, which is, in itself, a painful slap. Marie was my mother's name, a ghost I now carry around everywhere.

Caught, I slump down onto the loveseat. "I thought you were asleep." I sigh. It's not an apology. I'm fifteen, and I'm feeling particularly surly. The beer I drank with my friends earlier in the evening sloshes in my belly. I wonder if he can hear it. He does have very keen ears.

"You were wolfish," he accuses.

"I'm tired of pretending I'm something I'm not," I spit. "Just because you hate yourself doesn't mean I should, too."

"We've talked about this." With a flick of his wrist, his wheelchair edges closer. He rests his palm—grizzled and delineated by scars—on my bouncing knee. "It's not safe."

"Yeah, you keep saying that." I jerk away from his touch, pulling my knees to my chest. "But I'm not you. I'm not mom, either."

At the mention of my mother, his shoulders droop. There's a part of me that immediately regrets it; it's akin to setting him on fire just to warm my chilly hands. But, a larger part of me is indignant and wants him to hurt.

"You're suffocating me," I continue, adding kerosene to the flame.

I expect him to roll away, to reach into the cabinet for the bottle of Gordon's gin. The squarish bottle is his constant bedfellow. I expect him to shut himself in his room, and in the morning, I expect to heave him back into his chair and wipe the vomit from his chin.

Instead, his eyes—blue steel as sharp as paring knives—remain fixed on me. "Ama, a human shot me and now I cannot walk. Your mother is dead. You need to take this seriously."

"I can't hide," I manage. There's a lump in my throat. It's hard to look at him. It's hard to pretend to be grown up. "I won't."

"You will," my father says firmly. "I won't bury my daughter, too."

I think of the two of us standing graveside, the casket lid already covered in fallen leaves. The air was nippy, and I adjusted my father's blanket over his knees. He was dreadfully pale, his lips grey. He should have been at home, resting. Instead, he insisted we do this—and do it right. So, we stood vigil as the casket was lowered into the trench. I tossed a handful of dirt into the grave, like I'd seen in the movies, and he nodded approvingly.

"You aren't going to," I assure him. "I'm being very careful. Central Park was empty and—"

My father slams his fist on his armrest, making me jump. "No," he snarls. "No. This isn't up for discussion, Ama. We aren't wolves anymore. Not now, not ever. You are going to be a normal girl: finish school, get married, have kids."

I want to say no. I want to say, fuck you. *There's a lot I want to say, but instead, I grit my teeth and finally settle on: "I'm going to bed."*

I rise, stepping gingerly around his chair, but my father grabs my forearm and tugs.

"Look at me," he urges. When I meet his eyes, he offers me a wan smile. "I love you," he says. "I just want you to know that I love you." I wish I could tell him his love feels like a pair of shackles.

"Ama!" Flora bounds through the sand, bare-footed. She sits beside me, our shoulders touching. "I thought that was you. How are you feeling?" She's wearing a high-waisted skirt, her blouse tied just beneath her breasts. At her midriff, a diamond of tan skin is visible, burnished by the sun. Her heels dangle from her fingertips.

I probe my bandaged cheek with gentle fingers. "Not terrible," I reply. "It will leave a scar, though."

"Don't worry," Flora says, resting her chin on my shoulder. "You've got your new friend Flora to take care of that. I know a lady at Avon. I think you would look like a real dish in their prize pink lipstick."

"You're a lamb." I chuckle.

"Oh, by the way. Did the man find you?" she asks.

I give her a sidelong look. "Which man?"

"He's a guest at the motel. He said he knew you," Flora replies. "He was a dreamboat."

"I don't know who that could be," I say slowly. "Are you sure he's looking for *me*?"

Flora nods. "Of course, he asked for you by name. He's in Room Eight." She rises, wiping sand off of her thighs. "I'll see you later, okay? I promised Mags I would watch the pups so she can get a permanent wave at the salon."

After she leaves, I lay back in the sand, its warmth seeping into my limbs as I close my eyes. I mull over Flora's words. No one knows I'm in Wharton. I haven't spoken to anyone from the city since I left. Except—

I sit up, the blood draining from my face. *Could it be?*

♦ ♦ ♦

I stand outside Room Eight, staring at the door. I've almost knocked three different times, but I keep losing my nerve. *What if it's him?* I brush my fingers through my hair, trying in vain, to make it look less windblown. Surely, it can't be Bernard Edwards! Surely, it can't be.

Suddenly, the door flings open, and I jump back in fright.

Bernie, fresh-faced and clear-eyed, grins when he spots me standing awkwardly in the breezeway. He pulls me into a hug before I can even process what is happening, his arms encircling my thin waist. I wince as his shoulder bumps against my cheek. My body feels stiff. *What's wrong with me?*

Bernie holds me at arm's length. "I am so happy to see you!"

"Really?" I can't help but remember the way his face had contorted in fear when I showed him my true self. He had looked as though he could skewer me with the barbeque fork without a moment's hesitation. He hadn't, but it was apparent he wanted to.

I was—am—-an abomination. *No*, I amend. *Last night, I didn't feel like one. I felt free.*

"Of course," he says. "I've missed you."

"Really?" I feel like I'm underwater. *Oh, I may faint.*

"Ama." His brows knit together, concerned. "Come inside, are you okay?" His hand, starfished on my back, guides me into his room. I sink down onto the edge of the bed. "What happened to your face?"

"Why did you come?" I ask. My mouth is dry. My tongue sticks to the roof of my mouth.

"Well, for one: you didn't say goodbye," he says wryly.

"I'm sorry," I whisper.

"*And*," he continues, "I wanted to tell you something important." He kneels, until we are eye to eye. His eyes are just as beautiful as I remember: dark like the ground after a rainstorm. "Ama, I love you. I don't care what you are." He gently cups my face with his warm, calloused hands.

"But I'm—" I'm not entirely sure what to say, nor how to verbalize my tumultuous emotions tumbling inside of me. Rafe called me a wolf-girl. Which I suppose is what I am.

"I know," he insists. "Ama, I know there are *things* about you that are different."

"You remember?"

"Ama, listen to what I'm saying," he says, his tone impatient. "I want you to come home. I want to get married."

Am I dreaming? Is this a side effect of the whiskey Rafe poured down my throat last night, my trembling chin was cupped in his hand? He had insisted I drink it before he bandaged me up. *It'll hurt less*, he'd said.

"You want to be with me?" I murmur. "Even though, I'm..."

"Yes, darling. As long as it never happens again." He says it as though I made a mistake. That I transgressed. That I wronged him. I want to vomit, but—

Bernie strokes my hair, tucking it gently behind my ear. When he leans close and kisses me, I kiss him back. This is what I desperately wanted: normalcy. It's in my grasp. I can taste it on Bernie's tongue.

Slowly, Bernie clambers onto the bed with me, his hands unbuttoning my dress. In his haste, he pops a button. I can hear it ricochet off the dresser and land on the thin carpet with a muffled *plunk*. I run my palms down Bernie's back, shucking his shirt out of his pants, slipping my hands underneath. I could trace the constellations of his freckles with my eyes closed. I know his body so well.

"Marry me," he mumbles into my mouth. "I'm better. You can be better, too."

CHAPTER 8
(???)

———◁◆▷———

She checks into the hotel with her parents. Her father is a talker. During our transaction, I find out he's a banker, hailing from Wisconsin; this is their first time in Virginia, and there's a strong likelihood they will choose seafood for dinner, if I have any recommendations. She ignores me entirely, idly flipping through the rack of dog-eared and wrinkled brochures. No one ever takes them, and they are at least two years out of date.

"You're in Room Thirteen, two double beds," I say, "and I would recommend the seafood jambalaya at the little stand out on the pier. It's better than any restaurant, hands down."

After they head to their room, I step out front for a cigarette. It's early still—barely eight in the morning—and there's no one in the courtyard. I lean against the stucco wall, lighting a cigarette and taking a long drag.

"Hey." The teenaged girl stands some distance away, watching me.

"What can I do for you?" I ask.

"My parents wanted to see if y'all could spare any more shampoo," she says, shoving her hands into her pockets. She reminds me of an ungainly foal, its limbs far too long and much too frail. She stands awkwardly, knock-kneed and stilted, as if unsure what looks most attractive. Her hair is blond and stick-straight, just touching her bare shoulders.

"Sure," I reply. "Let me just finish this cigarette."

"Okay," she says, shrugging as if to say, *no skin off my nose*. "Can I get one of those?"

I wordlessly hand over a cigarette, lighting it for her with a flick of a match. She leans against the wall beside me, taking short little puffs. I wonder whether she's ever smoked before.

She smells strongly of perfume—something flowery, with an undertone reminiscent of an iced cupcake. Vanilla, maybe. She may as well have bathed in it, it is a cloying scent that overpowers even the smell of nicotine and tar. "How old are you?" I ask.

"Nineteen," she says without looking at me.

"Hm," I grunt.

"Yeah." She shrugs. "Is there anything actually *fun* to do in this town?"

"Depends," I reply. "Do you have a fake license?"

"No," she mumbles, crossing her arms over her chest.

"You're out of luck, then," I snicker. I drop my cigarette butt on the pavement, stubbing it out with my toe. "Let me get you that shampoo."

She watches from the window as I paw through the box of travel-sized toiletries we keep behind the desk. Now, she doesn't even pretend to smoke the cigarette, holding it loosely between her middle and ring fingers. She's very clearly interested in me.

I'm interested too, just not quite in the way she thinks.

"What's your name?" I ask when I step back outside. I hold out a small bottle of Halo shampoo. She plucks it from my fingers.

"Lucy," she replies. "Yours?"

"Rafe," I say, because it's the only name I can think of that's not mine. I'm not sure why I lie. It's not as though she'll have the opportunity to tell anyone. Surely, she won't relay this conversation to her parents. I will be her secret; she knows she shouldn't be batting her eyelashes at me. I'm a decade too old for her.

Her cigarette has burned down, several centimeters of ash drooping. "Maybe we could meet up later?" she asks, red blooms on her cheeks.

"Maybe," I say, trying to sound noncommittal. "I'll be on the pier. Come find me."

I lean back against the railing, my arms crossed over my chest. I hate to be on the pier in the summer. It's crowded and inordinately loud, especially when the fair is operating. Calliope music jangles from the speakers, while fairgoers shriek and cackle with unfettered delight. I almost don't hear her approach.

But I smell her. The smell of her perfume has dissipated somewhat, and beneath it, there's a heady, mouth-watering odor, earthy and roasty.

"Hey," she says, trying to appear casual. But her quavering voice betrays her. I cast my eyes about, searching for her parents. She must have noticed my lapsing attention, and she offers an explanation. "My parents went shopping. I told them I wanted to stay at the fair."

"I have a cooler of beer under the pier, if you'd like some," I say. My body thrums with wanting, and it takes everything in me not to leap atop her right here. *I'm so hungry.* It's becoming difficult to wait between kills. I find myself feeling sick more often than not; killing is the only medicine that quiets the churning in my belly, the pounding in my head.

"Sure," Lucy says, shrugging.

I lead her down the wooden stairs to the sand below, veering into the shadowy space beneath the pier itself. It's quieter here. The crashing tide replaces the sounds of mirth above. It's a dull roar, akin to the sound one hears when holding a conch shell against their ear. Is it really the sound of the ocean or just blood rushing through one's ear? I can never remember.

Lucy pauses and removes her sneakers, curling her toes into the sand. "Where's the beer?" she asks as we move deeper into the shadows. We skirt around algae- and graffiti-covered pylons.

"Nearly there," I tell her over my shoulder.

When I am sure we are alone, I turn and face her. Lucy bites her lower lip, casting her eyes to and fro. She's nervous now. She holds her shoes by their laces, and they dangle above the sand, casting a long shadow. "The beer?" she prompts. "Rafe—"

Chapter 8 (???)

"I'm sorry," I say, my voice throaty. "I really am." When she inevitably screams, no one hears.

CHAPTER 9
(RAFE)

I find myself making excuses to walk the breezeway when I know Ama is housekeeping. I often hear her voice wafting through doors left ajar, singing popular songs. Her favorite appears to be Doris Day. "My darling, my darling, I've wanted to call you my darling," she sings, humming when she can't remember the words. Sometimes, I even catch a glimpse of her. When she thinks no one is watching, she whirls around, her dress flaring around her knees.

But today, she isn't singing.

A man leans against the doorframe, watching her work. He is tall and slender, his hair a dusty blond. As I walk past, he makes eye contact with me. "Good morning," he says kindly.

"Are you bothering my housekeeper?" I ask.

He laughs, holding out a hand to shake. "I'm Bernard. Bernie. Ama is my girl." I want to crush every bone in his hand. He reeks of Acqua Di Selva aftershave. It's artificially woodsy, a spicy stink.

There's nothing underneath the smell of cologne—just meat. A human.

"Your girl?" I ask, looking past him, catching Ama's eye. She is in the middle of making the bed, the duvet bundled in her hands. I raise my eyebrows. She's never mentioned a man, certainly not a man who calls her "his." Except—

My fiancé. Ex.

Ama dumps the duvet on the bed, hurriedly spreading it across the mattress. Her cheeks redden as she works. I wonder if she can feel my eyes on her. Does it make her skin feel hot? "How many more rooms are left?" I ask her, nostrils flaring.

"Just this one," Ama replies. She plumps the pillows, hurriedly tossing them against the headboard.

"I need to see you in my office," I command. "After."

"Yes, sir," she mumbles. "Right away."

I offer the man a tight smile and stride back toward the front office. I'm fuming, though I'm not entirely sure why. Flora is at the desk when I shove open the door. "Why do you look like that?" she asks.

"Who's that man out there?" I ask. "The one with Ama."

Flora rises from behind the counter, craning her neck so she can see. "He's a guest in Room Eight. He was looking for Ama." She buffs her nails with a file. "Why? Are you jealous?"

From my vantage point, I can just see Ama in the doorway now, her hands resting on the doorjamb. She looks up into her visitor's face with a soft smile. He laughs at something she says and touches her hip with the tips of his fingers.

I avoid the question. "Send Ama in when she gets here."

I'm not alone in my office for long. I have enough time to roll up my sleeves and light a cigarette before Ama knocks, opening the door just enough to peek through. Her cheeks are flushed. "You wanted to see me?" There's a hint of mirth still evident in her voice. Clearly, her visitor has beguiled her.

"Come in and shut the door." Ama does as I ask, settling into the same chair she occupied when I bandaged her face, and, earlier when I hired her. "Who's the human?"

"My ex," she says slowly, her brow furrowed. "Why?"

"But he's a *human*."

"Is that a problem?" She looks genuinely confused, and I want to shake some sense into her. *Of course* it is! Humans can't be trusted.

"Man down, man down!" Anderson calls. Stifled by a volley of bullets and the scream of low-flying aircraft, it's unlikely anyone else has heard. Certainly, they didn't have time to pinpoint his location amidst the cacophony. But I can smell him, just upwind. I run, my feet tangling in the brush. Each step is its own little torment: my sunburnt flesh rubs against my flak jacket, my ill-fitted helmet jiggling on my head, and sweat dripping into my eyes with no way to wick it away.

Anderson kneels beside a soldier with a cherubic face. He can't be older than eighteen. His leg is sheared off just below the knee. He sobs. "I'm going to die, I'm going to die, oh God—"

"I can't carry him," Anderson shouts into my ear. "I can't carry him and keep pressure on this at the same time." He presses a pad of gauze against the soldier's leg, but it's not very effective. His Carlisle kit is strewn around him in a half-circle, the pamphlet torn.

The soldier is losing blood quickly, and his speech becomes slurred. "Gon'die, gon'die…"

I grab the soldier under the arms, hauling him up. But with his combat gear, he's too heavy, and we have to move slowly. Each step leaves more of his blood in the grass, and the nearest medics are tucked inside a trench a quarter mile away.

"We have to leave him," Anderson yells. "We're sitting ducks out here!"

"I'll take him." Before I can think it through, I shift into my wolfish form, tossing the soldier over my furred shoulder. It's the only solution I can think of. I can't let this kid die. "Cover me!" I command Anderson, but when I turn to look at him, his gun is pointing at my head. There are shouts from the Japanese too: Okami, Okami, Okami!

"Yes, it's a problem," I reply coolly. "I won't have a human putting my pack in danger."

"Bernie isn't like that," she replies, testy. "He says he doesn't care what I am." Her fingers toy with the loose threads of her helm.

"But—" I wheedle.

"But *nothing*. He accepts me."

I take a long drag of my cigarette, prowling around the room. Finally, I rest my hands on the arms of her chair, peering into her eyes. Her scent fills my nostrils, making me heady. "You're making a mistake," I murmur.

She huffs, her breath hot on my face. "Then, it's my mistake to make." She rises, pushing me away with a firm hand. "If you'll excuse me, *sir,* my shift is over."

♦ ♦ ♦

The Dock is quieter than usual. Most of its patrons are focused on the television, watching President Truman announce his plans to finance the Greek and Turkish military against the Communists ("I believe that we must assist free peoples to work out their own destinies in their own way"). I swallow the remainder of my whiskey, the liquid heat settling into my belly. My eyes are bleary, and I know this should be my last drink. Instead, I order another.

Samuel walks into the bar, bringing in a blast of wet heat with him. "Hey, pally," he says, sinking onto the stool beside mine. "You look like shit."

"Thanks," I reply dryly. There's something strange about Samuel tonight. He's nearly thrumming with energy, as though he's taken amphetamines. His eyes are wide and glassy. "Are you alright?" I ask.

"I'm great," he says, nonchalant. He gestures for the bartender to pour him a whiskey. "It's been a good night."

"Looks like you just had a shower," I observe. Samuel's hair is still wet, smelling strongly of hair tonic. "The night must just be getting started."

Samuel shrugs, tipping his whiskey down his throat in one swallow. He plunks 35 cents down on the mahogany bartop. "Something like that."

"You're leaving so soon?"

"Just gotta show my face." Samuel chuckles. "Say, how's the new girl working out? Elton said watching her take down that buck was *something.*"

"It was something, alright."

For a brief moment, I remember how Ama's body felt as she lay upon my back, gripping my neck tight. When she rested her cheek on my fur, I could feel her breath, fast and shaky. She was in so much pain, but she sat still when I washed and dressed her wound, never looking away from my face. Those eyes! Even wolfish, she disarmed me.

"She's either very brave or very stupid," he says. "Looks like she'll have a shiner for a while. Which is a shame for a dish who looks like *that*." He elbows me as though we are sharing a joke. But it just makes me bristle. "I've got to go, but have another drink on me, alright?" He presses a quarter into my hand, giving me a wink.

After finishing my drink, then another, thanks to my packmate, I meander toward home. I'm very drunk, and the ground seems to rush at me with each step I take. I turn onto Dorcett toward my apartment when I run into Ama. She is alone, carrying an armful of groceries from the pharmacy.

"Rafe!" she exclaims.

"Where's your fella?" I ask her. I am brash, unbeholden to social niceties. Though, I'm not quite tethered to them sober, either.

"I imagine he's in his hotel room," she says coolly.

"You deserve better," I blurt out. It's not quite the way I would have preferred to verbalize my feelings. But she deserves to run free like she did the other night. Surely, Bernie won't allow that. It's unseemly, beyond the pale, not becoming. Will she have a gun pointed at her head? Will she have to experience the waking nightmare of having to push him into the ocean, like I did the ensign?

Ama shifts her paper bag to her other arm, exasperated. "So you've said. Why do you care?"

"Because I care about you, wolf girl." We are standing in the middle of the sidewalk, and the crowd parts for us. We may as well be an island.

"You don't mean that, Rafe."

"I do," I reply, indignant.

"You're drunk."

"I am *very* drunk." I grasp her elbow, pulling her close. "But I do care about you. Come home with me."

CHAPTER 10
(AMA)

R afe's eyes are as dark as oil, and I find myself
mired in them. *Come home with me.* "Rafe,"
I say, weighing my words carefully. "You know I
can't do that."

"You can do whatever you'd like." He smells like
whiskey, medicinal and woodsy. And beneath it, the
earthen bouquet I've come to associate with woflish-
ness: damp fur, fresh air, and sulfur.

"What I'd like to do is go back to the motel," I reply
steadily. But, inwardly, I'm faltering. I love Bernie—
truly. Still, there's something drawing me toward this
man. When I ran beside him, nose to nose, I felt truly
unencumbered. When he carried me home and touched
my face with gentle hands, I felt safe. "Goodnight, Mr.
Blanchard," I add.

He's still standing so close. I could simply stand on
my tip-toes and kiss him. Instead, I turn away, walking
toward the motel. I don't look back.

When I arrive back at my room, I find Bernie inside, sprawled on the bed. He's watching *Winner Take All*. He grins when I place the bag on the small table, revealing the contents of our would-be dinner: bread, sandwich fixings, and a cylindrical tin of Lay's potato chips.

You deserve better. Surely, Rafe is underestimating Bernie, purely because he's human.

"Have I told you what it's like?" I sit on the edge of the bed, clutching the chip tin.

"What?" Bernie snags a chip, popping it into his mouth.

"Being a wolf. Hunting, running, any of it?" I am shaking. The television is so loud ("Do you want to be a winner? Then, sound your buzzer, sound your bell, and let's play *Winner Take All!*").

"Ama—" He sighs. "We talked about this."

"Did we?" I feel as though I've been punched in the gut. I feel stupid. What had I expected would happen?

"You aren't doing *that*. Not anymore." He says it so matter-of-factly. "You said you would be better."

"But," I whisper, "there's nothing wrong with me.'

Bernie sits up, taking the tin from my hands and setting it aside. "I know you can't help what you are. But I won't allow my wife to cavort through the forest or whatever it is you do."

"I'm not cavorting. I wish I could make this make sense to you. It feels like—"

"That's *enough*," Bernie interrupts firmly. "Ama, that's quite enough." His hand grasps mine, gripping tight.

Rising, I wrench my hand from his grasp. "I need to think about this. If I can't even talk about it, I...may as well be lobotomized."

I burst from the room, startling two men smoking cigarettes on the breezeway. I'm not sure where I'm heading until my heels sink into the sand, and I topple over. The ocean roars like a freight train. A storm is coming.

Pulling my knees up to my chest, I wrap my arms around them. The wind whips my hair back, my bobby pins no match for mother nature's bluster. Errant droplets pepper my skin, but I don't move. Let the rain come. I don't care anymore. I fantasize about the wind sweeping me up, tossing me from thermal to thermal. Maybe I'll be put down miles away, or maybe, I'll fly forever.

The beach is deserted. It's late, and the incoming storm has scattered even the die-hard beachcombers. I unbutton my dress, slipping it off of my shoulders. Then, I step into my fur. The joints in my fingers pop, curling backward until they touch my wrist. My shoulders jerk, the bones grinding. I open my mouth to cry out, but my tongue thickens, and it becomes hard to breathe.

Tonight, I welcome the pain. This is who I am. I am the woman who can endure this over, and over, and over. When my body finally settles, blood trickling down my lacerated cheek, I break into a loping run down the beach. I jog through the breakers, delighting in the cold splash of water tickling my belly. I pass a series of ramshackle bungalows and head into the dunes. Here, the sand is smooth, lacking the texture made by repeated footfalls. Tourists don't come here, amidst the sea grass. Tiny crabs skitter out from under my shadow, waving their claws as if to say *excuse me!*

Suddenly, I catch a whiff of something. It's a foul smell with a dash of cloying sweetness. I can nearly taste it, and I gag. The scent reminds me of a dead animal that's been left in the hot sun to rot, the skin shearing away from muscle and bone. I step closer, though everything in me tells me to turn away. There's something tangled in the seagrass, but it's far too dark to get a good look from this distance. When I kneel beside the lump and gently push the grass aside, I can't stifle the scream erupting from me, evolving into an anguished howl.

I burst into the front office, finding only Flora. At the sight of me, she leaps up from her stool, pulling me into her arms. I'm naked, shaking, fat tears intermingling with the blood on my cheek. Pink trickles edge down my breasts and over my flat belly.

In one fluid motion, she propels me into Rafe's office, hiding me from prying eyes. "Ama!" she exclaims. "What happened?"

"I saw a girl," I manage.

"A human saw you?" She grabs one of Rafe's left behind jackets, dressing me as though I'm a child. It still smells like him.

"No, she was dead. I saw a dead girl."

Flora pulls another chair close, sitting. "Where?" She reaches for the rotary phone, pulling the whole lot into her lap. The receiver joggles.

"The dunes on the north side."

Flora spins the rotary, dialing. I imagine she's calling the police, but instead, she says: "Rafe, you need to come down. No, not tomorrow. Now. Ama is here, she *found something*." After a moment of listening, she hangs up.

"We need to call the police, I think she was murdered," I insist.

"I know," Flora says slowly. "But I think this was one of ours. This isn't the first time."

CHAPTER 11
(RAFE)

◁◆▷

I find Ama—pale, her jaw set—in my office, Flora placing a mug of steaming coffee into her hands. Ama is wearing my jacket; it looks comically large on her, the shoulder pads slipping off her narrow frame. Flora's call was more sobering than a cold shower, and my head is pounding. "What's going on?"

"Tell him," Flora instructs, pouring two more cups of coffee. I politely take the proffered beverage, setting it on my desk.

"I saw a dead girl," Ama says, emotionless, "when I was running in the dunes."

"Are you sure?"

"Very sure, God, Rafe, the smell! Her neck was broken, and her stomach was…" Ama trails off, her face contorted. "It wasn't a stomach anymore. We should call the police, shouldn't we?"

In truth, I'm not entirely sure what we should do.

The missing persons posters plague me. *This is your fault,* their subjects say, speaking in one voice. *Why weren't you here to stop them?* I didn't do my duty—my due diligence—last year, and now there's another dead body, another missing person for the wall. The pack had assured me none of them were responsible for it. They convinced me the accusation was baseless, that I was projecting my own trauma onto them.

After all, how many planes had I shot down?

"I'll go check it out." I tell the two women. "And then I'll decide." Before going, I give Ama one last look. "Go home to your *fiancé*."

I follow Ama's scent, the divots made by her footfalls. In the dunes, I catch a whiff of garbage, and something akin to cologne. Death. I follow it, but ultimately find nothing: just a mess of crushed sea grass and churned sand. I circle the area, nose to the ground, trying to pick the smell back up, but to no avail. It's as though the supposed body had just dematerialized or been borne upward into the clouds.

The rain starts, fat droplets bursting on my muzzle. There's nothing to do now but head back home.

Sight unseen, I creep down the alley to my apartment, taking the back staircase to the loft. Only then do I step into my human flesh, gritting my teeth. It's late, nearly 3 o'clock, and I'm bone-weary. Naked, I crawl into bed, pulling the duvet tightly around my shoulders. I wonder, then, if Ama was seeing things. The smell was pungent, but it could have been a deer or a sea mammal. It's not unheard of for dolphins and the like to beach themselves. If she had made herself hysterical, she may have simply thought she saw something.

But, I think, Ama isn't the type. She wasn't over-wrought when she told me. She was hardly emotional at all.

Despite my restlessness—the unanswered questions—I fall asleep.

"Did I smell like that?" the ensign asks, sitting cross-legged on the edge of my bed.

"No," I reply, trying very hard not to look at him. There's a hole in his shoulder, through which I can see my end table and lamp shining brightly. Every wet muscle, every string of viscera is in sharp relief.

"And why was that?" he asks.

"Because it was only a minute. You were only dead for a minute."

"That's right," the ensign says, grinning. His teeth are pearly white in the lamplight. "You made sure of that, didn't you?"

Suddenly, I'm floating on my back in the ocean, the waves lapping over my arms and legs. I look up toward the side of the warship, at the figure peering over the railing. I recognize Ama, her hair wild around her shoulders, before a wave overtakes me, pushing me down into the ocean's darkest depths.

I can't breathe, I can't breathe, I can't...

I wake with a startling gasp. Cool air fills my lungs, and I nearly cry in relief. When I check the clock, it's one o'clock in the afternoon. I slip out of bed, dressing in a clean button-down and slacks. As I pull on my suit jacket, I can't help but to imagine Ama walking back to her room wearing mine. Did Bernie ask her whose it was, or where she had been?

As soon as I step outside, I freeze. It's as though someone—or something—has clapped its hands over my ears. Wharton is devoid of its usual soundscape. Where once there was joyous laughter and animated chatter, there is quietude. *Am I still dreaming?* I pinch the tissue-paper thin flesh on my wrist, wincing. *No, I'm awake.* I exit the alleyway, coming out onto Main near Seaside Books. The store is open, and there are people inside. There are also pedestrians on the street, walking to and fro.

But no one speaks above a whisper. It's the hushed tone reserved for funerals.

The owner of the bookstore, Edward Gold, steps out when he sees me loitering outside. "Have you heard?" he asks, wiping the sweat off his bald dome with a handkerchief. I shoot him a quizzical look. "There's a girl missing," he continues.

"Who?" A cold wave envelops me. Could it be Ama's dead girl reclining in the seagrass? I'd nearly convinced myself she was a figment of Ama's imagination, little more than hysterics and exhaustion commingling.

"A tourist. A young girl, maybe nineteen." Edward nods politely at a couple leaving his shop, clutching paper bags. When they are out of earshot, he leans close. "I am starting to think this town *is* cursed."

"It's starting to feel like it," I agree. "Hey, d'ya know where the girl was staying?"

"I think she was at your place," he replies. "Did no one call you?"

My stomach drops. "No," I reply. "I should head down there."

Edward starts to say something else, but I'm already speed-walking down the sidewalk. The three blocks to the Cove feel like they stretch on forever, and by the time the building comes into view, I've broken into a run. Three police cruisers idle outside, the red and blue turrets spinning lazily. Samuel and Elton are outside, speaking to the officers.

The Sheriff, a rotund man with a pinched face, looks up from his notepad at the sound of my feet on asphalt. "Mr. Blanchard," he drawls. "Nice of you to finally join us."

"No one called me, or else I'd have been here earlier," I assure him. "I only just heard about what happened. How can we help you, Sheriff?"

"Your manager gave me what I needed," the Sheriff replies, his tone chilly. He waves a crisply folded piece of paper, one I recognize from our ledger. "But, if you have any additional information you think is pertinent, I'd love to hear it."

"No sir," I reply smoothly, though inside, I feel anything but. "I'm just saddened to hear this has happened. That poor girl."

The Sheriff grunts, hooking a thumb through his belt loop. He stares at me, as if daring me to look away; only a guilty man would avert his eyes. I don't even blink, my eyes searing.

Finally, he gives me a terse nod. "We'll be in touch."

Samuel, Elton, and I watch silently as he trundles to his cruiser and climbs inside. As soon as his vehicle creeps out into the traffic on Main, I propel both men into the front office.

As soon as we pass through the threshold, Samuel wrenches his arm from my grasp. "What's the matter with you?" he grumbles.

"What's the matter with *me*?" I guffaw. "What's the matter with *you*? Speaking to the police? *Really*?"

"We didn't have much of a choice," Elton says. "What would you have had us do?"

"Call me!" I snarl. "Pick up the fucking phone! Ameche!"

"Oh, just like you gave us a heads up about the body?" Elton replies coolly. "I had to hear it from Flora *after* the news was going 'round about that missing girl."

I ignore his retort. "Now, I need you both to tell me the truth: did you kill that girl?" Elton looks as though I've slapped him. Samuel's eyebrows shoot up into his hairline.

"This is just like last year!" Samuel exclaims. "What a bum rap!" He leans against the counter, crossing his arms over his pigeon chest.

"I'm just asking," I say, sardonic. "After all, I was gone for six months, and a handful of people went missing."

"We had nothing to do with that," Elton insists. "C'mon Rafe."

"You're projecting," Samuel spits. "*You* were the one shooting the fucking Japanese."

Without thinking, I grab a fistful of his shirtfront, wrenching him toward me. Our noses nearly touch. His words are incendiary—meant to enrage me. I've shared very little with the pack about my time over-seas, but I've shared enough. There were a handful of nights we drank at The Dock, and I told macabre sto-ries that sobered them up real quick.

"What are you going to do, Alpha?" he asks sedately. It's as though I'm a joke. He looks at me through half-lidded eyes, a grin curling the corners of his mouth.

"Get back to work," I snap, releasing him. "Both of you."

CHAPTER 12
(AMA)

————◁◆▷————

"**I** have a surprise for you," Bernie says, waking me up with a gentle kiss on my sleep-creased cheek. The clock on the nightstand says it's late, nearly three in the afternoon. I sit up, tucking the bedsheets into my armpits to hide my nakedness. The memories of last night bubble to the surface, wetting my skin like perspiration.

"What is it?' I ask, my voice hoarse. I try very hard not to look at the cuff of Rafe's jacket peeking out from under the bed.

"Get dressed, sleepyhead," he cajoles, tugging on my wrists. "You've been asleep all day. This isn't like you."

I want to say: *all I can think about is a dead girl.* But instead, I nod. "I'll meet you outside," I tell him, "I just need a few minutes. Please."

"Alright." He sighs. "There's a commotion out front anyway. I'll go check it out." As soon as he's gone, I leap to my feet, throwing aside the comforter. I pull Rafe's jacket out from under the bed, trying to decide where to hide it where Bernie can't see. *You didn't do anything wrong,* I tell myself. *But still...*

I decide to hide it under the bathroom sink There are stacks of towels therein, and I can tuck it beneath them. As I fold the jacket, I can't help but catch a whiff of Rafe's scent. He smells so good, like a crisp autumn day after a downpour. Of the Earth. I hate how badly I want to press my nose to the fabric.

Before I can give in to the impulse, I stash the jacket, firmly shutting the cabinet. *I'll return it to Rafe later.*

I turn on the shower tap and wait for the water to warm. It feels good to step under the spray, scrubbing off the sand and sweat from the night before. I wish I could wash away the memories of the girl, the image of her body contorted and tangled in the seagrass. I wish I could forget her sightless eyes, staring skyward as if asking *why me?* I wish I could forget the wet hole that was once her stomach, the coil of her intestines in the sand. But, most of all, I wish I could forget the way she smelled: like meat.

Showering quickly, I slip into a fresh pair of under-wear and garters. I select a Kitty Foyle dress—dark blue with a white collar and capped sleeves. I pile my hair, still wet, into a chignon, covering the lot in a polka-dotted scarf. In the mirror, I am pale and har-ried, but there's no hiding it with makeup. Even Flora's Avon lady would have trouble. I settle for a dark lip-stick and a wet flourish of mascara.

Outside, Bernie is waiting, watching a group of men standing on the asphalt. One of the men is a police officer, the brim of his peaked hat casting a shadow over his eyes. I recognize the three men with him: Elton, in a Chambray shirt, denim pants and a pageboy cap jauntily tilted back; Samuel, in a pullover vest and slacks; and Rafe, in a button-down with the sleeves rolled up to his elbows. I try very hard not to notice his bulging forearms.

"What's going on?" I ask Bernie.

"I'm not sure," he replies. "Something about a missing woman. But don't worry your pretty little head about it. We have a nice day planned."

"Oh?" I can't peel my eyes away from the men. Rafe's posture is casual—dropped shoulders, hands in his pockets—but the others look tense. Samuel looks as though he might be sick. Elton is shifting from foot to foot, his jaw working.

"Come on," Bernie says, offering his elbow. "It will only be a short walk."

I allow him to lead me out of the parking lot and onto Main Street. He veers left onto the crowded pier. Groups of tourists try their luck at carnival games, eating candied apples, bags of Fritos, or French fries. "Just a little further," Bernie assures me. We leave the pier behind and walk along a gravel drive, passing squat bungalows in various states of disrepair. A street sign, askew, reads: Bird's Nest.

I know where we are. Beyond the houses, I can just make out the dunes. This is where I found the girl. For a brief moment, I fear that Bernie has found out, that he will take me straight to her. Instead, he brings me to a small bungalow, a FOR SALE sign held upright by cinderblocks. "What do you think?" he says.

"What do I think about what?" I ask.

"The house, knucklehead!" Bernie grabs my hand, dragging me up onto the porch. "I bought it. For us."

"You bought a house?"

"I bought *us* a house," he says. He produces a key from his pocket. "It needs a little work, but it's ours." He unlocks the front door, seemingly unaffected by my less than warm response. Inside, the air is stagnant, thick with dust. I can see the motes dancing in the sunlight. Cobwebs are draped across the rafters. "I know you wanted to live near the water," Bernie explains, "and this house was a *steal*."

Wordlessly, I walk through the house. The living room is painted blood red, white, lacy curtains still hanging in the windows. The kitchen cabinets are a pea green, some of which are missing, and, beyond the kitchen, a door leads outside onto a wooden deck.

I step outside, gulping fresh air. From here, the dunes are enormous—veritable mountains with valleys in which anything can hide. Is she still out there?

"Don't you like it?" There's an edge to Bernie's question. He's hurt.

"It's wonderful," I assure him. "It's just...a surprise." I can't peel my eyes away from the dunes. When I finally turn to look at Bernie, he's on one knee, a velveteen box in hand. Inside, there's the engagement ring he gave me before he shipped off: a solitaire diamond surrounded by gold filigree.

"Ama," he says. "I want to get married. I want us to have the life we dreamed of *before*—" Before the war. Before I showed him my truest self. *You can be better*, he'd said. That statement had rankled me, but there's also a tiny part of me that craves normalcy. Human

Ama would have never been out cavorting on the beach late last night, nor would she have caught the scent of the dead girl. Human Ama would have fallen asleep in her warm bed beside her boyfriend, rather than wearing another man's clothes and skulking around on the breezeway. "Will you marry me?" Bernie prompts.

"Yes," I say. "Yes, Bernie, I will marry you."

Bernie rises, slipping the ring onto my shaking finger. "I love you," he murmurs before pressing his lips against mine. This ring—this kiss—is an opportunity. I *can* be better. Normal.

CHAPTER 13
(RAFE)

I sit in my office, heels on the desktop, flipping through the *Tribune*. For the last few days, the front page has been clogged with stories about the missing girl. Her name was Lucy Carson. She was nineteen. She loved art and horseback riding. The paper writes about her in the past tense, salivating at the very idea that she is dead. They are desperate for a conclusion. Last year, they never got one. Already, they are connecting the cases. IS THERE A SERIAL KILLER IN WHARTON? IS THIS THE WORK OF A SUMMERTIME STRANGLER? THE SHERIFF WEIGHS IN!

I can't quite shake the feeling my packmates know more than they are willing to let on. But Samuel is right; perhaps it is little more than projection. I've seen the worst of what humans are capable of. I've killed men because I was ordered to do so. Men that knew my name, that sat across from me in the mess hall. Men that cried in my arms.

There's a soft knock at the door. "Come in," I call. Ama walks in, her housekeepers apron still tied around her waist. She is carrying my jacket.

"Mr. Blanchard," she says. "Can I have a moment of your time?"

"Sure," I reply, taking my feet off my desk and putting my paper aside. The last time we spoke I was so dismissive of her. But she was right, wasn't she? "I wanted to talk to you, too."

"Oh?" She sits, placing my jacket on her lap. Her fingers fiddle with the buttons.

"I wanted to apologize," I say. "The other night I was very rude."

"You were anxious," she says, shrugging. "I was, too. But that wasn't what I wanted to talk about. What I wanted to say is I'm quitting my job here at the motel. I—"

"Why?" I ask. The thought of her leaving is like a punch in the gut, a sweep of the leg.

"Bernie and I are engaged. He doesn't want me to keep working," she says, averting her eyes. For the first time, I notice the ostentatious ring on her finger. *Stupid girl.* She had told me herself: Bernie could never accept the wolfish part of her. She frightened him.

"Are you returning to New York?" I ask, gritting my teeth, trying to hold back the angry words itching to burst forth. I fear if I start, I will not stop, that I will reveal my true feelings and hurt her's.

"No." She finally meets my eyes again. "Bernie bought a house on Bird's Nest."

I laugh. "He bought a dump. Jesus, Ama, you—"

She rises, stepping around my desk to hand me my jacket. "I just wanted you to know," she says. "Good bye, Mr. Blanchard." I ignore the jacket, grasping her wrist instead.

"You're making a mistake," I tell her. "What are you going to do? Never be a wolf again? Be some housewife and push out babies that will never know what they are?"

"Yes," she says, *not* trying to free her hand from my grasp. "Yes, I deserve to feel the tiniest bit of happiness. He and I were happy before—"

"Before you showed him," I finish for her. "You deserve someone who sees all of you. Someone who *wants* all of you."

She laughs humorlessly. "And who would want that? I'm a fucking monster." Tears well in her eyes, and she sniffles. "Let go of me, Rafe."

"You aren't a monster," I tell her. I don't let go. I know that if I do, she'll leave, and I'll never see her again. I can't stand the thought of it. I rise, so that we are mere inches apart. "Don't do this."

"He wants me," she says firmly.

"I want you," I say before I lose my nerve. "I want you, wolf-girl." I cup the back of her neck, pressing my lips to her's. Her lips part, and I press my tongue inside, delighting when she responds in kind. *God, she tastes so good.* My hands slide down her back, cupping the twin globes of her ass. "Stay with me," I murmur into her mouth. Her body presses up against mine.

When I finally release her hand, her arms encircle my neck, keeping me close. She is the first to break the kiss, her eyes half-lidded.

"We can't," she whispers. "Oh, Rafe, we can't."

I kiss her cheek, her jaw, her neck. "We can," I purr. Gently, so very gently, I nip at the sensitive skin there. She gasps, her fingers tangling in my hair.

Another knock at the door forces us to pull apart. Ama wraps her arms around herself, taking several steps back. Her cheeks are ruddy, and her lipstick is smeared. Nico peeks his head into the room. "Rafe, a customer—"

"Not now," I snap.

"There's a ceiling leak in Room Fifteen," he says. "This can't wait."

I sigh, scraping my hair back. "I'm coming. Get them moved into another room. I'll check out Fifteen." When Nico does as I ask, he leaves the door ajar. "Ama—" I say, but she just shakes her head.

"I need to go," she whispers.

"I don't accept your resignation," I reply, wiping a bit of her lipstick from my mouth with the pad of my thumb.

"I don't need you to," she says. "Good bye, Mr. Blanchard."

Before I can say another word, she turns on her heel and leaves.

"Look who the cat dragged in," Elton crows, waving animatedly at me from a booth. He mimes throwing a lasso over me, reeling me in. I roll my eyes, but head toward him. I had planned to drink alone, but

The Dock is teeming with tourists looking for a cheap thrill and an even cheaper drink.

Elton and Mags are cuddled up in the booth, sharing a bench, while I take the bench opposite, resting my elbows on the tabletop.

"You look like shit," Elton observes, pouring me a beer from his pitcher.

"Elton!" Mags admonishes him.

"He knows I'm joking," Elton snaps, none too kindly. "Right, Rafe?"

I grunt, noncommittal, and take a sip of the foamy beer.

"We heard Ama quit," Mags says. Her eyes search mine, as if looking for some clue as to what had happened. I shrug my shoulders. "I know you liked her, Rafe, I'm sorry—"

"Rafe doesn't like anyone," Elton snickers. "Least of all himself."

I cross my arms, surveying my brother. "Do you have something to say?" I ask him. Elton is clearly in a mood. He's been abrasive for months now, angling for confrontation.

"No, no, I'm just fucking with you," he replies.

"He's had a lot to drink," Mags says as an apology.

It is then I notice the dark bags under her eyes. She looks exhausted. Could the pups be keeping her awake at night? "How are the girls?" I ask.

"They're fine," Elton says, waving away the question. "What happened with the housekeeper?"

"She's getting married," I reply, taking a gulp of my beer. The outside of the glass is slick with moisture, making my palm damp. I wipe them on my pant legs. "Apparently, she's moving out to one of those bungalows on the north side." Saying it aloud makes my stomach ache. I can still feel the ghost of her lips on mine.

Mags' brow wrinkles. "I thought for sure she was running from something when she arrived in Wharton." Mags had told me about that night at the diner, of the dog-tired woman in a wrinkled dress who ordered a coffee and a recommendation.

"Yeah." I sigh. "I thought so too. But, maybe, she was looking for it to chase her." I can't help but imagine Ama in her new home at Bird's Nest, the curve of her smile pressed against her fiancé's shoulder as they slow dance in the kitchen. But she had kissed me back, hadn't she?

"C'mon, Rafe," Elton slurs. "You have your pick of women, and time to pick them all. Why are you so grumpy?"

He's right. But I don't know how to explain it.

I could go home with a stranger tonight. And tomorrow night, too. I've been with a lot of women since my return from Japan. But they were just warm bodies, a nightlight to keep the ghosts at bay. Ama, I think, might have been a beacon.

Instead, I ask him, "How did you know Mags was the one?"

Elton wraps an arm around his wife. "When she had our first child in her belly," he chortles.

"*Elton*," Mags groans. She's clearly heard this joke before.

"I knew when she was the only one I wanted to see when I woke up," Elton says, when his laughter finally abates. "It was the first—and only—time I ever rolled over after a date and thought, 'golly, I'm glad she's here.'"

"Then he took me to breakfast," Mags adds. "We sat on a bench near the beach and shared a bag of donut holes."

It is easy to imagine them sitting on that bench, both awkwardly dipping their hands into the same paper bag. Did they chuckle when their fingers inevitably touched and the powdered sugar freckled their laps? Without any effort, I can imagine Ama and I in their place, her freckled face upturned toward the sun.

"So, that housekeeper gave you the brush up?" Elton asks. "Sounds like she's a hot cake."

The accusation makes me bristle. Ama certainly wasn't juggling Bernie and I. "You've got it wrong," I reply, unable to sheath the edge in my voice.

My brother takes a swig of his beer. "You'll find another one," he assures me. "Maybe someone a little less *impulsive*."

Impulsive? I suppose. Her decision to marry did seem abrupt. One minute, she was describing their relationship as incompatible, irreparable. But now, their engagement is back on. "Maybe," I reply, noncommittal.

"Don't you remember how she took down that deer?" Elton asks despite my lack of enthusiasm; he wants to keep talking about Ama. "If she had used her head, she wouldn't have gotten hurt."

I think of Ama's lean, milky-colored body streaking past me like a missile, her blue eyes focused on her prey. Despite the animal's sheer size and the keen antlers atop his head, she was impetuous. *Is she approaching Bernie with the same short-sightedness, the same haste? Will it be just as painful with no consolation prize?*

Elton gestures to the waitress for another pitcher. Mags sighs, and he scowls at her. But then, he turns his attention back to me. "Does this mean we have to take turns doing the housekeeping again?"

"I'll handle it," I say glumly. "Flora can put an ad in the paper and hire a replacement."

As we drink the second pitcher, Elton's body loosens. He slumps in his seat. His voice becomes thick, slurred with spittle arcing from his lips. He's very drunk. "We should be getting home," Mags says. "Flora can't stay with the girls all night."

"She can wait a lil' longer," Elton replies abruptly. "Don't be a nag, Margaret."

Mags rises from the bench, her jaw set. "I'm going, then. You can find your own way home."

"I'll get him home," I assure her. "Or, he can stay at the apartment."

"I can take care o' myself," Elton adds, glaring at his wife.

"Suit yourself," Mags snorts. She turns, her skirt flaring around her knees. "I won't wait up," she calls over her shoulder, her hand raised in a flippant wave — a flag of surrender.

Later, Elton and I walk down the street, the hot air enveloping us in its moist embrace. Sweat drips down my back, made worse by Elton's arm draped over my shoulders. "Y'know," he mumbles. "It's been good t' spend time t'gether, just us."

I nod in agreement. We had a lighthearted conversation over our second—and later, our third—pitcher. For a moment, I had even forgotten about my heartache. "Just like old times."

"God, I'm hungry," Elton groans as we pass the diner. He pauses, gazing into the picture window. His eyes rest on a group sitting at a 4-top, chatting and eating an array of finger foods. One of the men—slender and olive-skinned with dark freckles adorning his nose—notices us and gives us a quizzical look. I look away, but Elton isn't dissuaded. He may as well be salivating over their spread: Coney dogs, fries piled high with melted cheese, and frosty glasses of Coca-Cola.

"I have chips at the apartment," I say, tugging at his arm. "C'mon."

Finally, Elton allows me to lead him away and down the alley. "We could have feasted like *K*ings," he whines. "The taste is unreal. You have to try it."

He must be more inebriated than I thought. I've eaten at that diner plenty of times. In fact, we were both there, together, just last week.

CHAPTER 14
(AMA)

The house on Bird's Nest is a cacophony of sound. Bernie has been in the living room, hammering up art deco cornices since dawn. The radio is on, Nellie Lutcher and her jazz trumpets playing throughout the house. I step around the dust cloths on the ground, heading into the kitchen to brew a cup of coffee.

"Am I being too loud?" Bernie asks, wiping the dust off his denim coveralls.

"Very," I reply. I've been in a foul mood since I quit my job, since Rafe kissed me in his office. Now, everything Bernie does is an annoyance. He's too loud, too quiet, too needy, too distant. Too, too, too—

I'm being unfair. "I'm sorry, my love, I just have a headache," I say.

"You've been having a lot of headaches lately," he observes, his bushy eyebrows knitted together in concern. "Maybe you should see a doctor."

"No, no," I assure him. "I just need a cup of coffee and some fresh air."

"Why don't you head down to the beach?" Bernie suggests. "You haven't been since we've moved in."

The image of the dead girl flashes before my eyes. Will I see her again? Sometimes, at night, I imagine her outside the window, dragging her chipped nails along the window pane.

"Maybe," I reply.

There's a fresh pot of coffee in the kitchen, and I pour myself a cup. I look out the back window at the deck, and beyond it, the expanse of sand and sea. A seagull has landed on the deck railing and surveys me with one large eye. I give the bird a little wave, and it launches itself into the air, startled.

Suddenly, the music is replaced by the tinny voice of the local newsman. "A man, Freddy Parnell, aged 25, confesses to the murder of missing woman Lucy Carson and the five unsolved missing persons from 1946: Greta Thorpe, Gerry Calhoun, Ernesto Balthazar, Denise Fletcher, and Sheila Sparks. Parnell is being held in James River Correctional Center." So, that's her name: Lucy. I thought it would feel better to know who she was, but, now I just feel *sad* for her. She was only nineteen years old, and she died with her guts piled in the sand. *That poor girl!*

"Maybe I will go for a walk," I call over my shoulder. "I'll be back later."

Bernie grunts in response, his hammer striking wood with a resounding pum, pum, pum.

I leave my untouched coffee on the counter and head out back. The deck wobbles under my bare feet. It's one of the many things on Bernie's repair list. At least it will keep him busy. He often falls asleep on the couch just after sundown, snoring. In a way, it's a relief. I worry my body will betray me and shy away from his touch. After Rafe's kiss weeks ago, my stomach has been in knots.

Kissing Rafe was unlike kissing Bernie. It was passionate, dangerous. It was akin to the feeling I had leaping atop that buck, sinking my teeth into the creature's warm flesh despite the frantic swinging of its antlers. I walk down to the waterline, wincing as the icy cold water sweeps over my toes. From here, I can see the pier, and beyond it, the copper dome atop the courthouse, now a sickly green color.

Since moving to the bungalow, I've hardly seen anyone but Bernie. He bought an old truck, and we drive into town to visit the hardware or grocery store. But he's been so preoccupied with house repairs we never stay out for long. I haven't even seen the Cove. But perhaps, it's for the best. Now, I'm not as tempted to be wolfish. I have no one to run with—or *to*.

I sigh, and sit in the sand, watching the tiny sand crabs scuttle around me. To them, I'm nothing more than an obstacle, a mountain blocking their way. Sometimes, that's what Bernie feels like to me: an obstacle. But I haven't the heart to go around or over him.

It's for the best, I remind myself. *He used to be all you wanted*. But I also thought he was different. I thought he would see me in my fur and still love me. I thought he would be there when I came home from a hunt, eager to hear all the glorious details. Instead, he left without a kiss goodbye, walking straight into a battlefield because it was more palatable than I was.

I can't help but think of Rafe's gentle hands as he patched my face. I touch the scar there, still pink and raised. He thought I was brave. When I tried to tell Bernie the story, he scoffed. "See?" he'd said. "That life is far too dangerous for you." Any mention of wolfishness is met with a shake of the head or an exasperated, "Ama, please. We discussed this."

I miss that part of myself. Desperately.

I want to run. I want to feel the wind ruffle my fur and the sun warming my shoulders. I want to smell the earth and read the cues only the flora and fauna are privy to. I look around me, but just as it was when I walked down here, the beach is vacant. The only people who use this part of the beach are crabbers, and they work in the very early morning. Right now, their traps are back in the water, the buoys bobbing on the surface.

I slowly unbutton my dress, casting it aside. I unclasp my bra, placing it on top. Then, my underwear and garter. For a moment, I simply stand on the shoreline, the crabs crawling over my feet. *Should I?*

Yes.

My shoulder blades spasm and tip backward, stretching my skin. My ears tip forward, the ocean waves deafening. My skin tingles, fur coursing over my ribs. As my pelvis narrows, I lose my balance, falling forward onto my hands—my paws. Moments later, I regain my footing, sitting back on my massive haunches. The pain is excruciating, but it ebbs quickly, as it always does.

Then, I run.

For a mile, I follow the shoreline, the last few bungalows passing on my left flank. When the shoreline abruptly veers into an inlet, I trade the soft sand for rougher terrain. There are no people out here, just forests. Here and there, I find a hunting blind, but they are unoccupied. It will be months before it is deer season in Virginia.

I run until I catch her scent. It's a doe, nibbling at some undergrowth near a fallen tree. I slowly ease onto my belly, not wanting to startle her. She seems completely unaware of me; she doesn't raise her head, and while her ears swivel, she doesn't point them in my direction.

Salvia pools in my mouth. I shift my weight.

A leaf crunches beneath my foot, and the doe lurches away. She leaps over the fallen tree, bounding away as fast as her cloven hooves can carry her. She's quick, but so am I. I easily shorten the distance between us, following her white plume tail through the thick forest. I leap for her, and close my jaws on—

—empty air. *Damn*.

The deer veers right, her legs akimbo. I skid, overcorrect, and nearly run into a low-hanging tree branch. Thinking quickly, I duck and slide, regaining my feet on the other side of it. The doe is within arm's reach, and I grab her back leg with my big paw, giving her a jerk backward.

She is fragile, and I feel her femur break in my grasp. I sink my teeth into the back of her haunch, lacerating the femoral artery.

"Care to share?"

Startled, I turn to see a large black wolf, his lips pulled away from his gums in a gruesome amalgamation of a smile. "Rafe?"

"Good to see you, Ama," he replies coolly. He sniffs at my kill. Hearing his voice, even this version of it, makes my stomach churn. I can't help but think of that moment in his office, his hot breath on my neck, his hands grasping my ass.

He wrenches a piece of meat off the doe's side, chewing. Blood trickles down his chin.

I don't have an appetite anymore. I am in dangerous territory. I'm not supposed to be out here in this body. And I'm certainly not supposed to be here with another man.

"Aren't you going to eat?" Rafe asks, his mouth full.

"I'm not hungry anymore," I manage.

He slurps up a sliver of gelatinous fat, surveying me. "Ama, we don't waste food. That's a pack rule."

"I'm not in your pack," I reply coolly.

He chuckles in his deep timbre. His fur melts into his pores, and his tapered snout reconstructs into his handsome, squarish jaw. He opens and closes his mouth, the bones popping. When he is fully human, he puts his hands on his hips. It looks like Rafe hasn't shaved since I've seen him. He has a short beard, and his hair is more unruly than ever. I try very hard not to stare at his nakedness, but it's difficult not to. He is subtly muscular with a tapered waist and thighs as thick as tree trunks. His cock hangs heavily between his legs.

He reaches up and strokes my muzzle with his gentle hand. His touch is like a balm on my weary body. I've felt so terribly alone. I've felt like a slice of a person: a cross-section of my most boring, most palatable parts.

"Rafe," I whimper, stepping out of my fur, too.

He keeps his hands on me as I transform, so when I'm done, he's cupping my chin. "Where have you been, wolf-girl?" he asks.

"Bird's Nest," I manage. "With Bernie."

"Are you happy?" Rafe asks.

It's a simple question without a simple answer. There are tiny moments of happiness with Bernie: drinking coffee on the deck, laughing while we paint the cabinets, and waking him up with his favorite breakfast—bacon and eggs. But I'm not entirely happy. I knew that from the minute I said yes the first time. He didn't even compare to a routine run through the forest, my wolven heart hammering in an excited staccato.

"No," I finally say, resting my palm against Rafe's bare chest. "But he—"

"Let me make you happy," Rafe murmurs, cupping my neck.

I'm trembling. Tentative, I reach up and touch his face, my thumb glancing off of his bottom lip. It feels like we are the only two people in the world, or at least, the only two people for several miles.

Rafe ensnares my lips with his, kissing me with the same gusto as that day in his office. His muscular arms encircle my waist, pulling me firmly against his naked body. His cock is already hardening, pressing against my hip.

Suddenly, he lifts me off my feet, carrying me away from my kill. I squeak in surprise, wrapping my legs around his waist and my arms around his neck. When he sets me down moments later, we are in a small clearing, no larger than the length of our bodies. It's as though the space was made for us—for this moment.

Gently, Rafe lays me back on the soft grass, his kisses trailing down my neck. "Let me make you happy," he repeats, his tongue hot against my skin. "Say 'yes.'"

I tangle my fingers in his hair. If I do this, there's no going back. I can't simply shrug on the mantle of a happy, dutiful housewife, who makes her husband breakfast. I won't be able to look at Bernie in the eye again, much less marry him. *God, I'm a horrible person.*

Rafe's hot breath is on my breast now. His tongue snakes out to lick my hardening nipple.

"Yes," I finally say. "Please, Rafe."

Rafe sucks my nipple into his mouth, giving the sensitive skin there a nip. I whine, arching my back. His kisses descend to my belly, the firm edge of my hipbone, the tops of my thighs in turn. When his tongue drags along my sex, I whimper, bucking my hips. *More, more, more!* With gentle but firm hands, he spreads my legs wide, circling the sensitive pink nub there with his tongue.

I feel flayed open, every nerve-ending singing.

He rises from between my legs, kissing my mouth. I can taste myself on him: earthy and semi-sweet. His cock presses against my thigh, precum dribbling. "Are you sure?' he asks, breathless.

I am very sure. I want him in every conceivable way. Thoughts of Bernie, the dead girl, all of it, evaporate, floating back toward the troposphere. "Please," I moan. "Rafe, please."

With that, he presses his cock inside of me. He groans, his body shaking. He is trying to be careful, gentle. But I'm his wolf-girl, and I don't need it. I raise my hips to meet him.

He grasps my breast in one hand, using the other to hold himself upright. "You feel so good," he murmurs, lascivious. Suddenly, he pulls out of me, leaving my skin tingling and wanting. "Hands and knees," he commands.

I do as he asks, fisting the soil beneath my palms. I may as well have grown roots, becoming as tall and immoveable as the trees that surround us. Rafe's cock presses into me, and he leans over my back to kiss my shoulder.

Rafe thrusts into me, contentedly growling into my ear. Suddenly, his body stiffens, and he gasps, thrusting hard, over and over and over. He forgets to be gentle, his fingernails leaving divots in my skin. He pulls out, translucent cum still dripping from his vascular cock. "God," he groans, brushing his hair out of his eyes.

I turn to face him, sitting on my heels.

What happens now? I want to ask, but instead, he pulls me onto his lap, expertly bringing me to orgasm with his hands.

CHAPTER 15
(RAFE)

◁◆▷

I t's getting late. The sky—barely visible through the canopy—is pink, the sun starting its descent below the horizon. Ama lays beside me on the forest floor, her arm draped over my waist and her breath hot on my shoulder. She's asleep; the worry lines on her face are soft, nearly imperceptible. We both need to return to the real world, but for the moment, I dilly-dally.

When the sky turns violet, I rouse her. "The sun is going down."

She sits up, looking skyward. "Oh no, he's probably worried sick."

He. Bernard Edwards. Her *fiancé*.

"Come home with me," I cajole, gently tugging her down atop me.

She nuzzles my earlobe. "I need to end it," she murmurs. "Even if, you and I—" She looks down at my face, her hair draped over her shoulder. "Even if this is nothing, it's not fair to him."

"I don't want this to be nothing," I assure her, stroking her soft cheek. "I want to be with you." I've been intimate with a lot of women—human and wolfish alike—and none of them have made me feel the way Ama does. No one has delighted me, frightened me, or intrigued me as much. She even quiets the voice of the ensign who always whispers in my ear.

She leans close and kisses me on the lips. It's chaste, and in it, there's a goodbye. "Can I come by the motel, after?" she asks. "I'll need a room."

"Of course."

Still straddling my hips, she transforms into her wolfish form. Her hands grip mine tightly, her fingernails painfully digging into my palms. When her body settles, she looks down at me with startlingly blue eyes. "Later," she assures me, licking my cheek with her long, flat tongue. Then, she is gone, loping through the forest.

I wait for the sounds of her to fade before I sit up and stretch.

My body feels loose and warm, contentment settling into every muscle. When I transform, the pain is far away, barely registering. I settle into an easy gallop, heading toward the lights of Wharton. When I reach the water tower, the sky is dark. I change into the clothes I left there, finding the dress Ama had worn weeks ago, sopping wet on the ground. I squeeze the water out of the fabric and take it with me; surely, she will want it later.

I stroll into town toward the motel, the dress draped over my arm. It still smells like her. Or, do I smell like her?

When I reach the front office, I pause outside. Elton and Mags are fighting, their voices hushed. But with the door ajar and the light turned on inside, I can hear and see them. I'm not sure what possesses me to listen in. Perhaps it's Mags frantic tone, or the fire burning in my brother's narrowed eyes:

"You're being stupid," Mags says.

The pups—Delia and Carla—play with dolls on the carpeted floor. Carla, the youngest at two, looks bizarre with wolfish ears and fur sprouting across her jaw. She snarls at her sister, tugging a doll out of the other girl's hands.

"You need to stop," Mags says to Elton. "You can't keep doing this to—"

"Shut your trap," Elton snaps, his voice rising. Both children look up at their father.

Mags grasps his arm. "Keep your voice down," she hisses. She gives the girls a tight smile, waiting for their attention to wane. Delia, sensing the tension, grasps her sister's hand.

"Let's go into Uncle Rafe's office. He always has candy in his desk drawer." She urges her sister up. Once they are out of earshot, Mags turns her attention back to her husband.

"Rafe will find out," she warns.

"He won't find out," Elton snorts. "He's always somewhere else—in his head." He circles his finger around his ear, the sign for *cuckoo, bonkers, cock-eyed*. I take a staggering step away from the office door. It's as though my brother has swept my legs from under me.

He thinks I'm crazy? And what the hell *is he hiding from me?*

"Don't worry your pretty little head about it," Elton continues. He cups his wife's chin in his hand, pulling her mouth to his. "Take the kids home."

Mags sighs and calls for the girls. Both obediently bound to her side with wet mouths full of bright pink Bazooka bubble gum. She picks up Carla, balancing the toddler on her hip, and takes Delia's hand. "Say 'goodnight' to daddy, girls," she says, her tone pinched.

"Goodnight, daddy," Delia parrots.

"'Night!" Carla shouts.

Before Mags can see me loitering outside, I step into the alcove, out of sight. The ice machine hums. As soon as her footfalls and the girls' chattering dissipates, I head into the office. Elton, sitting at the front desk, tips his chin. "Where have you been all day?" he asks, his voice betraying nothing.

"Hunting," I reply coolly.

Elton stretches, tilting his chair back on its hind legs. "Did you hear about the arrest?"

"Arrest?" I rest my elbows on the counter, appraising him. *What is he keeping from me?* Or rather, *what haven't I noticed?*

"They found the guy who took that girl," he replies. "It was the Parnell kid. Can you believe it?"

Freddy.

I know Freddy. He's a tall, lanky fellow with persistent acne on his chin. He wears denim every day, no matter the weather. His cat, Mara, often sits on The Dock's terrace, waiting for her master to finish his gin rickey and handful of pork crackling.

Freddy would never hurt a soul. Or, so I thought.

"Freddy killed her?" Something about this revelation doesn't sit right with me. How could Freddy have possibly carried off the girl, leaving no trace behind between Ama's discovery and my subsequent search? There were no drag marks, no dried blood, not even an indentation in the sand.

"The five from last year too," Elton adds, lighting a cigarette. "Looks like *someone* needs to apologize to Samuel."

"I didn't accuse anyone."

"Not directly." Elton scoffs. "But you didn't give him the benefit of the doubt either."

"At least it's solved," I say, clapping his shoulder and giving him an affectionate shake. I know he's angling for a fight, but I don't want to have one. Nothing will ruin what has become a perfect day.

Even his mysterious conversation with Mags feels wholly unimportant.

CHAPTER 16
(AMA)

I find my clothes on the beach, just where I had left them. I dress quickly, my heart hammering. Now that I'm out of the forest, the spell has been broken. I've made a mistake, haven't I? My core feels empty, as though I am little more than a doll stuffed with straw. It's a level of emptiness I am unaccustomed to. I feel as though I may puke.

As soon as I step onto the porch, Bernie flings the door open. He roughly pulls me inside, slamming the door so hard the frame rattles. "Where the hell were you?" he snaps, squeezing my arm tight.

I'm not sure what to say. "I'm sorry," I manage. I catch the briefest glimpse of myself in the small circular mirror hanging in the hallway. I'm dirt-streaked, my hair frizzy and loose around my shoulders. "I didn't mean to worry you."

"You did it, didn't you? You were a...*wolf*." He hisses the last word. *You can be better*, he'd said, as though wolfishness is a pox that must be inoculated for. I try to step away from him, but his grip tightens. "You promised me."

"I can't," I say. "I can't promise it. I was wrong to even think I could. Bernie, it's—" His knuckles connect with my jaw, wrenching my head sharply to the right. The pain takes a moment to register, but when it does, it's a deep burn.

"I'm so sorry," Bernie says, his hands to his mouth. "Oh god, Ama, I'm so sorry. I didn't mean to—"

I gently touch the spot on my cheek and wince. "Get out of my house," I say coolly. "Go back to New York."

"C'mon, Ama, you don't mean it." He reaches for me, his arms wide, but I step out of the circle of his embrace.

"Get out before I kill *you*," I say, louder now. "Get out before I rip your *fucking* throat out." Paresthesia crawls up my neck, coursing over my scalp. My hearing is suddenly heightened, and I swear I can hear Bernie's heartbeat: quick as a hare's when it is frightened from its burrow. I can feel his regret dripping off him, leaking from his pores like oil. It smells just as foul. "Out!" I scream, clenching my fists at my sides.

Bernie opens his mouth to argue but thinks better of it. "I'll get a room in town, we can talk tomorrow," he chatters.

"You'll be in New York tomorrow, and I'll send a box with your things," I correct him.

Bernie sighs, mopping his brow with his sleeve. "You're making a mistake."

"I have nothing left to say to you." I step around him, grabbing a bunch of his clothes and shoving them into his Army duffel. He just watches me, slack-jawed. I press the whole lot against his chest. "Get out."

He slings the strap over his shoulder. "Ama—"

"As soon as you told me I was a monster, I should have been done." My teeth crowd my mouth, making it difficult to talk. I'm trying very hard to hold my wolfishness in check, but I'm losing control. *Get out of the house, Bernie*, I scream inwardly. "Go," I manage as my tongue swells. Bernie's eyes bulge as my body takes up more space in the tiny foyer. My dress tears. "Get out!" I roar.

Finally, he does as I ask. He fumbles with the doorknob, whimpering, then bursts into the night, racing toward his truck. He stumbles, scrabbles in the gravel but regains his footing again. He drops the keys and blindly searches for them in the dark; the light from the open doorway doesn't quite reach him.

He looks absurd, like an Abbott and Costello gag.

When he finally makes it into the car and starts the engine, I shut the door.

Cloistered inside, my body settles; any hint of wolfishness trickles away. It is only then the tears come, and behind them, the heaving sobs. I sink to the floor, my back pressing against the door, and cry until I lose my breath. I've known for some time that my relationship with Bernie was doomed, but I never thought he would hit me.

Finally, the tears abate, and a new feeling replaces the abject sadness: detachment. Calmly, I rise, toss my ruined dress into the kitchen trash can, change into shorties, and crawl into bed.

I don't even bother to turn the lights off.

♦ ♦ ♦

Knock, knock, knock!

I wake with a start, tossing the duvet aside as though it's an enemy intending to attack me. "Who is it?" I call, my voice thick with sleep.

"It's Flora!"

I rise, tugging on my shorties, doing so as though it will make them look more presentable for guests.

When I finally open the front door, Flora grins. She's wearing a floral-print peplum dress, the sleeves wide like bird's wings. "So," she says, drawing the word out like *soooooo*. "A little birdie told me you might be returning to work."

I'm not sure how to respond. I step aside so she can come in. "I'm going to make coffee," I say. "Would you like some?"

"Sure." Flora brushes past me, examining the small bungalow. "This place is just *darling*. Where's that big, strapping man who lives here with you?"

"He doesn't live here anymore." I touch my chin, palpating the edges of the bruise there.

Flora shrieks, taking my head in her hands, tilting it so she has a better view. "Did he do that?" Her eyebrows knit together, her face serious. "Did you eat him?"

I can't help but laugh. "No. I kicked him out."

"Well, that's good," she says brightly. "Now, about that coffee."

I put the percolator on the stove and flip on the burner. Flora plops down at the kitchen table, smoothing her dress on her lap. "A little birdie told me my friend might be returning to work, and I wanted to see if it was true. Y'know, before I got too excited."

"Who told you that?"

"No one *told* me," she replies. "But my *nose* did." She taps the tip of her button nose with her manicured nail. "I could smell you."

"You could smell *me*?"

"On Rafe. I figured you had a chat. He seemed like he was in a good mood. Y'know, he was a real sour-puss after you quit." When I hand her a cup of coffee, she blows on the steaming liquid, creating gentle ripples on the surface.

"Something like that," I reply, hiding my grin behind my coffee mug.

Flora is silent for a moment, dragging her finger around the rim of her cup. "I also wanted to ask you about the girl. The one in the dunes."

I can't help but look out the window at the heaps of sand cresting the horizon like the interlaid coils of a dozing snake. "What about her?" I ask.

"I was trying to remember what you had said about her stomach."

"Her stomach? Why?" I sit across from Flora, examining my friend's face for any hint as to what she's thinking.

"Just humor me, okay?"

"Well." I sip my coffee. "It was very dark, but I thought it looked like her stomach had been ripped open."

"Yes, that's what I thought you'd said." Flora presses her lips together. "I was just watching the news coverage, and I'm not sure that little, skinny man could have *done* that."

"Surely, many humans are capable," I muse. "Think of that horrible Albert Fish fellow."

"Sure," Flora shudders, thinking about the so-called Werewolf of Wysteria, a man who murdered and consumed children. "I just don't think Freddy is capable. He bags groceries, for god's sake."

She takes a prolonged sip of her coffee. "He also got rid of the body very quickly, didn't he? There was no trace of her when Rafe went. Not even a bit of blood."

"What are you getting at?"

"I think—" Flora sighs, resting her chin on her palm. "I think she might have been killed by someone in the pack. Rafe suspected as much last year."

I lean close. "Who?"

"Rafe thought it was Samuel. But I'm not sure I disagree."

I think of the quiet, greasy man who trudges through the motel. He is often skulking around the breezeway or pushing a lawnmower out front. I've never spoken to him so much as heard him grunt. He grunts when he passes me on the breezeway, or when he's interacting with a guest. He's completed whole transactions without saying a single word.

"I don't know much about Samuel," I finally say.

"There's nothing to know," Flora says. "Sam is... *Sam*. He's quiet, a bit of a loner." Her lip twitches, as if trying to decide whether to grin or frown. "To tell you the truth, I'm sort of frightened of him."

"Do you have a reason to believe it's *him*?" I'm fascinated.

"Rafe came back from Japan last summer, after the others went missing. Rafe thought it was one of us. He came into the front office, fresh off the boat, teeth bared. Sam was the only one who got on his case about the accusation."

"That must have been a shock," I muse, "for an Alpha to accuse his packmates."

She shrugs her thin shoulders. The sleeves of her dress flutter. "Rafe is a loose cannon on his best day. I wasn't very offended. I knew I didn't do any-thing wrong."

"Were the others upset?"

Flora sucks her teeth. "I'm not sure. Elton came inside looking like he'd been kicked in the balls. He'd picked Rafe up from the shipyard out in Norfolk. Mags was sort of flabbergasted, I think. Nico was upset, but not angry—not like Sam."

"But Freddy confessed."

Flora tugs on one of her curls. "I know, which is why I don't want to say anything. I'm starting to think I'm going nuts."

"I don't think you're nuts," I assure her.

Abruptly, Flora rises. "I should go. I have an appointment at the salon before my shift starts. If I don't leave now, I'll lose time under the heat lamp. When are you starting back?"

"I haven't actually asked for my job back," I admit.

"But Rafe, you—" Flora raises her eyebrows. "Ama! Oh, Ama, you naughty thing! Don't tell me, you're—"

"Hurry," I remind her. "You'll be late."

CHAPTER 17
(RAFE)

R ight after Flora shows up for her shift, her hair newly coiffed into a stylish pompadour, I excuse myself. I'm tired of sitting in the motel, torturing myself with a myriad of *what ifs*. Ama never showed up at the motel: not the night of our tryst, nor the day following. *Is she regretting it?*

"Heading home?" Flora asks, a wide grin traversing her face. She looks like the cat who ate the canary.

"Something like that," I reply, evasive, shrugging on my pinstriped suit jacket. I can feel her eyes boring into my back. "Why?"

"Oh, no reason," she says. "I just thought maybe you were going to visit Ama." Flora sits at the counter, crossing her legs, one shoe barely hanging onto her toes. There's a hole in her stocking, but she doesn't seem to notice.

I scoff. "Why would I do that?"

"Y'know, her *fiancé* moved out," Flora drawls, giving nothing away. "She sent him packing."

I don't reply, but inside, my heart soars. Perhaps she hadn't changed her mind after all. I certainly haven't changed mine. *I want her*—desperately. I've gotten one little taste, and I'm ravenous. "Get to work, Flora," I tell my packmate.

"Sure thing, boss," she replies cheerfully.

It's warm outside, and I sweat beneath my suit jacket. Poolside, Nico waves. It's his day off, but a group of young people have caught his eye. They seem just as enchanted by him. They giggle, flapping their eyelashes, showing off by turning somersaults underwater, kicking their legs like pistons. Nico leaps in to join them.

I find Elton's truck in the lot, the keys tucked behind the visor. He's repairing the leaky faucet in Room Three, and he has other tasks besides. He'll be busy for hours. It's hotter inside the vehicle, and I inadvertently sit on a stuffed bear, presumably belonging to Carla. The engine starts with a hacking cough, and I pull out onto Main Street.

I pass the courthouse and notice the missing persons posters have been removed overnight. Instead, they've been replaced by posters demanding justice and vilifying Freddy Parnell. A crowd has gathered there, too. I can't tell if they are celebrating or mourning. Perhaps both.

Main Street itself is busy; tourists and townies alike are enjoying the temperate weather. It's nearly July, and days like this are rare. Typically, it's so hot the air is thick. I wave to some of my neighbors and friends, feeling uncharacteristically cheerful. *Ama left Bernie!*

I'm not quite sure where Ama lives on Bird's Nest.
I drive slow, windows down, trying to catch her scent
with my human nose. But all I can smell is the ocean.
Most of the bungalows appear abandoned, many
sporting FOR SALE signs. I find only three with resi-
dents. One, its siding powder blue, has a name on the
mailbox, and it's neither Edwards nor Chilton. The
second, its roof nearly slipping off of its eaves, has a
dog chained outside, barking at my vehicle as I creep
past. The third house must be hers: it's freshly painted
a peachy pink, and the front porch is decorated with
large urn-shaped planters, stuffed with spiderwort.

I park and sit behind the wheel for some time. The
car becomes hotter and hotter, and I awkwardly take
off my jacket, tossing it into the passenger seat. To tell
the truth: I'm nervous. It's one thing to meet up in the
forest, half-wolfish, half-uninhibited. But here?

Finally, I mount the porch, rolling my shirtsleeves
up to my elbows. When I knock, my stomach flip-
flops. Ama answers within two quick breaths, her eyes
bright and her lips parted in surprise. "Rafe," she says.
"Come in."

She steps back, and I cross the threshold. The
bungalow is small, but smartly decorated. It's not
aggressively beachy, a motif most Whartonites favor.
Instead, it's painted in muted earth tones with only a
few mementos here and there: a sand dollar, a dried up
starfish, and a cluster of shells in a jar.

There are photos on the walls, too, but I try not to
look at them. In one, Bernie grins in his Army dress,
Ama tucked under his arm like a trophy.

I turn to Ama, who despite the late hour, is still dressed in silken shorties. The pajamas leave very little to the imagination. Then, I notice the bruise on her face. It's a brilliant red with a corona of purple. "What happened?" I ask, forgetting myself and cupping her face between my palms. "Did he do that to you?"

"It's nothing," she mumbles.

"I'll kill him," I growl.

She reaches up, touching the knuckles of my hand. "He's gone. If he comes back, *I'll* kill him." She smiles, tightly. I can't tell if she's joking or not. I'm certainly not. I want to rip his throat to shreds until his apologies turn to incoherent gargles.

I drop my hands, squeezing them into fists. "I'm so sorry this happened, it's my fault, I—"

"He was angry because I was wolfish," she says. "He didn't—doesn't—know about...us." *Us*. I like the sound of *us*. She reaches for my hand, entangling her fingers with mine. "Were you telling the truth in the woods? That you want to be with me?"

"Yes," I say without hesitation. "Look, Ama, I'm not a perfect man. I am flawed. But with you, I feel so good."

"Me too," she whispers. "I feel good, too." Slowly, excruciatingly so, she steps closer, standing on tiptoe to kiss me. I cup the back of her neck, gently holding her there. For a moment, her body presses against mine. The fabric of her pajamas is so thin, and I can feel every curve of her. When we pull apart, she looks up at me with hooded eyes. "Do you want to see my bedroom?" she asks, coquettish.

"I was thinking of fucking you in the foyer," I admit, running my hands down the curve of her spine, slipping beneath the waistband of her shorts.

"Rafe Blanchard!" Ama huffs. "I'm a *lady*."

"I never said you weren't," I snicker, kissing those pouty lips again. "I just want you — desperately."

"Come with me," she insists, leading the way to the back of the bungalow. *I want to see what is under those shorts.*

The bedroom is bright, the windows offering natural light in spades. The bed is relatively small but looks cozy. She has an inordinate number of pillows piled against the headboard. She sits on the edge of the bed, looking up at me.

Slowly, I unbutton my shirt, letting it fall to the ground at my feet. Then, I pull my tucked undershirt out of my waistband, shucking it up over my head. Ama unabashedly watches me, her breath quickening.

I don't want to leave her waiting. I take off my belt, not bothering to pull it from the loops. Instead, I unbutton and unzip my pants, letting them fall around my ankles. My underwear is all that is left. Ama reaches for me, cupping my stiffening cock through the increasingly restrictive fabric. I gather her hair up in my fist, stroking the curve of her skull with my knuckles.

"Please," I whisper.

She hooks her fingers into the waistband of my briefs, pulling them down my thighs. My cock springs free. Her little pink tongue eases from her mouth, tasting me. *God.* It takes everything in me to not press into her mouth. Instead, I wait. Her cheeks turn pink, and she looks up at me, unsure. Then, she takes me into her hot mouth.

"Ama," I sigh, tightening my grip on her hair. "That feels so good." I try to be gentle, soft. My muscles twang, bunching like a coiled spring. I want to devour her. I watch her lips stretch to accommodate me, her long eyelashes fluttering against her rosy cheeks.

When the flat of her tongue swirls around my sensitive head, I gasp. "Let me kiss you," I urge, gently pressing her back into the mattress. Beneath me, she is pliable, raising her hips up to meet mine. Her fingers drag through my short beard, pulling my face into the hollow of her neck. I kiss her there, then sink my teeth in.

Ama yowls, arching her back so our hips grind together. "Rafe!" she moans.

I reach between us and push her shorts down, rubbing my palm against her wetness.

She whimpers, her nails dragging down my shoulders. "Please," she says, just like I had earlier. *Please kiss me. Please fuck me. Please love me. Please, please, please.*

I raise myself up onto my palms so I can watch her face. Ama's eyes meet mine—a sapphire whirlpool I am more than happy to drown in. When I slide into her, her lips tremble, her breath hitches. She cups my neck, pulls me close, and sinks her sharp teeth into the flesh of my shoulder.

"There you are, wolf-girl." I chuckle, the pain like a bolt of lightning throughout my entire body. Even my toes tingle. Then, the tingle courses back up my body, thick black fur sprouting in its wake.

CHAPTER 18
(AMA)

I wake in the middle of the night, desperate for a drink of water. Rafe is naked beside me, sleeping on his stomach. He softly snores. I sit up, leaning close to press my lips against his shoulder, just above the indentation of my teeth.

I pad naked into the kitchen, retrieving a glass from the cabinet. I fill it from the tap, taking a sip. My body is sore. Sex with Rafe was carnal, unabashed and wholly uncomplicated. It was not so much "making love" as it was "rutting." His wolfish teeth left scars on my neck, my breasts, my thighs. He is similarly marked by my mine. While the wounds will inevitably fade, what is left behind is indelible, written in invisible ink. It's as though we are tattooed on each other now.

I climb back into bed, trying very hard not to wake him. But Rafe's eyes—two shining opals, a predator's eyes—are open. "Hey," he murmurs.

"Go back to sleep, wolf-boy," I tell him, curling up against his heat.

His smile presses against my shoulder. "I was just thinking," he says, "about the night you found the girl."

"Oh." I fear I am cursed to never go a day without thinking of her. Those empty eyes, staring up at the heavens! It had been such a beautiful night before the storm rolled in.

"I was awful to you that night," he continues. "I wanted to say...I'm sorry." *Go back to your fiancé,* he'd spat, as though I was a nuisance. He may as well have kicked me like a stray dog. "You didn't deserve that."

"I didn't," I agree.

Rafe's arms slip around my waist. "I told you I'm not a perfect man," he says. "I'm not even a good man. But that night, I should have been there for you. I should have believed you."

I run my fingers through his hair, picking the knots apart. "You're a good man, Rafe. Truly."

"In Japan," he says, "I wasn't. I was awful." He props himself up on his elbow, looking down at me. "That's what I'm getting at. I'm *used* to seeing that. Living that. But you aren't, nor should you be. I should have been more—" Rafe pauses, as if searching for the word. He touches my lower lip with his thumb, grinning when I slip my tongue out to lick him. "—empathetic. I thought you were overreacting."

"She looked awful," I admit. "I can't get it out of my head."

Rafe says nothing, merely lays back beside me, burying his face in the curve of my neck. He peppers kisses on the flesh there.

I think of the conversation Flora and I had earlier. "Do you think that man did it?" I ask.

"He confessed," Rafe replies.

"I know," I murmur. "But she was *brutalized*, Rafe. Whoever—whatever—has done this...took a bite out of her."

For a long moment, he is silent. His breath is hot on my neck, even and slow. "What are you thinking?"

"I *think* he isn't the guy, is all. Unless he's one of us."

"He isn't," Rafe replies. "I know him. He's human. You think a wolf did this?"

"I don't know." I sigh. "She was eaten, I know that. Her intestines were..." I trail off, squeezing my eyes shut. I don't want to describe it. I'm afraid that if I say it aloud, I will inadvertently conjure her ghost. I can almost see her in the room, standing over my bed. Her belly is flayed open, her entrails tangled around her bare feet. *No, no!*

"Last year," Rafe says, "I accused the pack of murdering those people. But Freddy confessed to those, too."

"He did," I agree. "Maybe I'm just being silly."

Rafe doesn't say anything. Instead, he pulls the blankets up over our heads, his teeth grazing against my nipple. We don't talk anymore.

♦ ♦ ♦

BAM! BAM! BAM!

I burst awake, my arms pinwheeling. *Who's there?* I rub my eyes. For a brief moment, the room is hazy. I rapidly blink it away.

Rafe stirs beside me, mumbling.

"Open up, Ama!" *Bernie*. Stupid man. "I won't let you do this," he shouts. *BAM! BAM! BAM!*

Rafe sits up, reaching for his discarded clothes and pulling them on. "Let me answer the door," he says. "I would love to speak to him." A grin traverses his face. He's delighted at the prospect.

"I don't need you to protect me," I remind him. I rise, opening my armoire to find something to wear. I don't bother with undergarments, merely pulling a pea green McCardell playsuit on, cinching the waist. I'm determined to get to the door before Rafe does.

"I have no doubt that you don't," Rafe replies. "I would just very much like to have a chat with him." He looks pointedly at the bruise on my chin, the periphery having turned a sickly yellow overnight.

We reach the doorway at the same moment and briefly tussle. It's friendly, both of us snickering. I get out first, being smaller and more nimble. "Stay here!" I say over my shoulder.

BAM! BAM! "Open the door, woman!" And then: "You bitch."

"What a meatball," Rafe growls. "Let me open the door."

"Stay!" I command. Rafe steps back into my bedroom, huffing. Then, I open the front door.

Bernie is red-faced and shaking, his anger palpable. "This is *my* house, and you're *my* girl. I'm not letting you throw me out."

"You hit me," I reply coolly. "I'm certainly not *yours*." This new Bernie—indignant, brutish—is wholly unlike the Bernie I fell in love with all those years ago. *When had this transformation occurred? Was it when he saw me rise up, head and shoulders above him, my teeth shiny and keen? Or when I stood up to him, unwilling to change myself to suit his needs?*

"Let me in," Bernie pushes past me, his shoulder spinning me around.

"Get out of my house," I insist. My voice is louder than I intend, a growl beneath the words.

"I'm not leaving," Bernie says. He turns to face me, his fists clenched. His knuckles blanch white.

"Are you going to hit me?" I ask serenely.

Bernie shakes, his jaw tight. "Stop fighting me on this, Ama. We are meant to be together. We've always been meant to be together." I know he's thinking of the way we met.

I was in secretarial school, learning such skills as the attractive arranging of papers, and he was an Army private. We met purely by accident, colliding in a stairwell.

"Oh!" I exclaim, my armful of papers jettisoning from my hands. They flutter through the air like butterflies.

"I'm so sorry," the man says, trying to catch them. "My fault." He's handsome, dressed smartly in his pressed, khaki uniform. His garrison cap has fallen to the ground, previously tucked in his armpit.

I kneel to retrieve his hat, smoothing it. "No," I assure him. "I wasn't watching where I was going. This stairwell is always empty. I didn't expect to see anyone here."

He chases one of my documents down to the landing below, trotting back up to hand it to me. Our fingers touch. "I'm Bernard," he says, breathless. "Bernie."

"I'm Ama," I reply, suddenly shy. I pat my cheeks, as if I can quell the burn. "Nice to meet you."

"Say," Bernie says, "let me make it up to you. Would you like to get dinner tonight? I know a great Chinese place—their chop suey is amazing."

"I would love that," I reply.

"This is ridiculous," I say. "Just get out. I'm done. There's no going back."

"No," Bernie says, indignant. "You can't give up on us. I won't allow this." He grasps my arm, squeezing right.

"You're hurting me," I say slowly. I'm preternaturally calm. I'm not frightened of him.

CHAPTER 19
(RAFE)

I am trying very hard to respect Ama's desire to confront Bernie alone. But, when she says *you're hurting me*, I step toward the doorway without thinking. Bernie, drawn to the flash of movement, turns to look at me. "What is he doing here?" he snarls.

"I'm the person who's going to beat your face in." I step into the living room. Ama wrenches her arm out of Bernie's grasp. The afterimage of his fingers remain on her flesh.

"Rafe," Ama says, a warning.

"Your *boss?*" Bernie exclaims, a guffaw bursting forth. "You're fucking your boss?"

"I don't have to explain myself to you," Ama says coolly. "Just get out of my house. Go home." I am struck by her bravery. Even human, she exudes a sort of confidence that is undeniable.

Bernie bristles, his eyes boring into mine. "Do you know what she is?" he spits. "Did she show you? She's a monster."

"Careful who you call a monster." I chuckle. "I can show you a monster, if you'd like."

"Leave," Ama says, planting her palm against Bernie's chest and pushing him toward the door. "Now." He allows himself to be moved.

"She's a wolf! She's a fucking wolf!" he shouts. "She'll ruin your fucking life—like she did mine."

I can feel my teeth crowd my mouth, my tongue swell. I have to breathe through my nose. When I open my mouth to speak, my tongue lolls out. When my zygomatic bones crackle, the sound akin to a fire-work, Bernie gasps. "You two deserve each other," he manages.

Ama steps away from him, her fingers brushing against mine. Her cool touch settles me, and I swallow hard. Bernie throws open the front door, stomping down the patio stairs. When he flings the door of his truck open, my facial bones fuse back together. "He's going," Ama whispers.

"He's going," I repeat, if only to reassure myself. I want to give chase, to tear the bumper off his vehicle with my teeth. I want to leap into the bed and smash the glass of the cab, wrenching him out. I want to devour him as the truck careens down the street, rudderless. He would taste so good, just like—

—I can see the ensign out of the corner of my eye, standing beside a polyester armchair. *I tasted good, didn't I?* he hissed. I squeeze my eyes shut, and when I open them again, he's gone.

When the sounds of Bernie's truck diminish, Ama shuts the front door. "I told you to stay hidden," she admonishes me, but in a gentle tone. She's not angry.

137

"I couldn't help it, I didn't want that stupid man to hurt someone I care about." She wraps her arms around my waist, her cheek against my chest. I drop my chin to kiss the top of her head. "I know you could hold your own, but I couldn't sit idly by."

"He's gone now," she says, choking out a sob. "He's gone." Her tears wet my shirt. "I feel just terrible."

"Ama." I stroke her silky hair. "He called you a 'monster.' He hit you."

"I know," she insists. "I just wonder if I didn't try hard enough. I wonder if I could have put my wolfishness aside—hid it in some closet. Maybe I didn't love him enough."

"That's preposterous." I hate the mental gymnastics she has had to perform. I sorely wish I could wipe that from her memory and leave her only with the freedom afforded by her wolven form. "You did more than your fair share, darling." When she unbuttons my shirt, I know that, for now, she is done talking.

When we approach the motel, we are both sluggish, leaning into each other as if our bodies cannot bear to be apart. Ama and I fit together so well, it seems a shame to have to exist as two separate beings. "What's going on?" Ama asks.

The motel is a veritable beehive. Guests swarm into and out of the front office, their rooms, and into the over-chlorinated pool; I can smell the harsh chemicals from here. Elton, Mags, and Samuel loiter outside the front office. Through the window, I can just barely see the slope of Flora's frizzy pompadour as she checks in guests. While summertime is busy at the Cove, we aren't usually this busy unless it's a holiday weekend.

Elton spots us. His brow furrows slightly. I can almost hear what he's thinking: *Stupid Rafe. He's going to cost us the housekeeper yet again because he can't keep his cock in his pants!* It wouldn't be the first time. But he doesn't comment on it. "We're full up," he says. "There isn't a room available in the building."

"Freddy Parnell's trial starts tomorrow," Mags adds, puffing on a cigarette. "I think these are all reporters."

"Lots of camera bags," Samuel grunts.

"Let's get to work, then," I say.

Ama slips out from under my arm, her cheeks a blotchy red, and trots toward the utility shed to get her cleaning supplies. Samuel follows her, muttering about needing to empty the pool filters.

Elton surveys me. "The housekeeper?" he asks. "Isn't she married?"

"No," I snort. "She isn't."

"Well, her not-husband was here looking for her this morning," he says. "He wasn't very kind to Flora."

"He found her," I say wryly. "He won't be a problem. Not anymore."

Mags sighs. "Please don't hurt that girl, Rafe. She's sweet."

"What sort of man do you think I am?" I'm a bit hurt by their accusation, even if they aren't saying it outright.

"The kind of man who loves 'em and leaves 'em," Elton replies, taking the cigarette from his wife and taking a drag.

"Broody," Mags adds.

Suddenly, our conversation is interrupted by a scream from the utility shed. Ama bursts from the building, her face pale and her eyes wide. The shed door strikes the opposite wall with a loud retort, making her throw her arms over her head as if expecting an attack. The sound makes me reflexively flatten against the stucco wall, expecting mortar fire.

When Samuel follows Ama from the shed, his forearms are soaked in blood.

CHAPTER 20
(AMA)

The shed has one dangling lightbulb. One must reach for it blindly, waving one's hand through the pall. Even with the door open, the light barely penetrates the umbra therein, as if the shadows are somehow corporeal. I hate the shed; I often worry someone will grab me before I can switch on the light. When the light is on, however, the shed loses most of its eeriness. It's just a shed: packed corner to corner with the tools of the trade. There's a lawnmower; the push cart in which I pile used towels; a small, gas powered dinghy; several canisters of gasoline; pool supplies, strongly smelling of solvents and chlorine; and a lone folding chair, where, sometimes, Samuel dozes off.

I reach for the light, toes barely passing the threshold. But then, Samuel reaches over my shoulder, clicking it on. He smells rank, like old sweat. "There you go," he says breezily, brushing past me to get to the pool supplies.

"Thanks," I murmur. I'm about to pull my cart out of the shed when I hear her. At first, I think I've imagined it, but no: a tiny voice saying *he-he-help*. "Is someone in here?" I ask Samuel, craning my neck to see into the darkest crevices. There are a lot of spaces where someone could hide, and even, where someone could get inadvertently trapped.

Could a guest have wandered in? The shed hadn't been locked.

"What are you talking about?" Samuel asks. He hadn't heard it.

Help. There! I've heard it again! I pull aside my cart and start to move the lawnmower. It makes a sickly squeaking noise on the concrete, the plastic scraping. A woman is on the floor, curled up in the fetal position. Her wrists and ankles are banded together with army green duct tape.

"Jesus!" Samuel fishes a pocketknife from his coveralls, using it to saw the thick tape.

"What happened?" I ask the woman, kneeling beside Samuel. The big man shakes like a leaf muttering *Jesus, Jesus, holy mother of—*

"He—" she manages before her eyelids ease shut. When Samuel rips the tape from her bruised wrists, we both recoil. There's a wound in her belly, much like the one I saw on the woman in the dunes, albeit not so deep. The blood has made a dark pool on the concrete.

Samuel presses his hands into the woman's stomach, trying, in vain, to stop the bleeding. "She's dead," I cry. "She's dead. Oh, oh God, Sam, she's dead." I lurch to my feet, feeling as though I may be sick. The air in the shed is stagnant, and I can't inhale any air that isn't hot, that doesn't smell like blood.

I burst from the shed, wailing, and Samuel follows. The sudden brightness hurts my eyes, and I wince, throwing my forearm up to shield them from the onslaught.

Arms wrap around me, and I blindly bat at my attacker. "Ama!" Rafe says. "It's me, it's me!" His big hand encircles my wrists, pulling me tight against his chest. "Tell me what happened."

"There's a girl in there," I manage. "Dead."

Samuel wipes at the blood on his arms, making a high-pitched keening sound. "No, no, no," he cries. "Not again."

Elton grabs Sam in a bear hug, walking him backward into the shed. "Guests can't see you," he snaps when Samuel attempts to fight him off. "Inside."

Rafe walks me in, too. When he closes the door, the four of us huddle together under the lightbulb. "What happened?" Rafe asks, his tone firm.

I wordlessly point into the mire of industrial metal, within which the girl is barely visible. "We found her," I whisper. "She was alive for a moment—just a moment."

Rafe releases me, and I feel as though I'm in danger of floating into the atmosphere where I will inevitably *pop* like a helium balloon. *I may as well*, I think. *I don't want to be here*. I can't look at the girl again.

Rafe kneels where I've pointed, gently moving a bit of old wrought iron fencing aside. "Who did this?" He rises, whirling on Samuel. "Was this you?"

Samuel, sallow-faced, gasps. "I tried to save her." He holds up his hands, smeared with blood. "Maybe Freddy—"

"Freddy has been in jail for days. How many times have *you* been in and out of this shed since then?" Rafe's anger rolls off him in waves. We all try to duck under them, but instead, we drown in it.

I want out of the shed. I want to gulp fresh air.

"Rafe, I need to get out," I moan. "I can't be here."

Rafe isn't listening. He's grabbed the bib of Samuel's overalls into his fist, giving the other man a violent shake. "Did you do this, you creepy fuck?"

"No!" Samuel pushes Rafe away. "No, I didn't. Maybe speak to your *fucking* brother."

Elton laughs. "Don't you dare turn this around on me. We've caught you red-handed." Samuel turns, slapping Elton with his open palm. The blood creates a handprint on the side of his face.

"This isn't a fucking joke," Samuel snarls. "You've gotten away with this for long enough."

"Enough!" Rafe shouts. "Both of you. *Enough.*"

The floor spins beneath my feet, and I reach out for the side of the laundry cart. The wheels, unlocked, shift, and the ground flies up to catch me. For the briefest moment, before I lose consciousness, I meet the dead girl's eyes. Hers are blue, just like mine.

I wake on the floor in Rafe's office, his jacket tucked under my head. Rafe sits at his desk, a cigarette dangling from between his lips. He's pale, paler than

I've ever seen him. I slowly sit up, and for a second, the world tilts on its axis. But, after a breath, everything stabilizes. Grey motes dance in the corners of my vision.

Rafe notices me stirring and leaps to his feet to assist me. "Ama," he says around his cigarette. "How are you feeling?"

"I'm—" *I'm not sure.*

Rafe helps me into a chair, retrieving his jacket and draping it around my shoulders. "You've been out for a while."

"How did I get here?" I think of the hundreds of guests on the property, many of whom had cameras. *Will I be on the news tonight? How about the girl in the shed?*

"Mags pulled the fire alarm," Rafe says. "It gave us a few minutes to sneak you in, sight unseen. I didn't want you to wake up there."

"Where's the girl?"

"Still where you found her, the poor thing." Rafe rubs his eyes with the heels of his hands, his jaw grinding together. I notice the glass ashtray is full of cigarette butts. Rafe smells strongly of smoke. "I'm not sure what to do," he adds, the words seemingly bitter on his tongue as he spits them out.

"Shouldn't we call someone?" I ask. "The police?"

"It's complicated." Rafe leans against his desk. "If it *was* Samuel, we could be exposed."

"Samuel seemed just as surprised as I was," I say slowly. "Surely it wasn't him."

"Sam is a complicated man." Rafe stubs out his cigarette. "He's always been."

CHAPTER 21
(RAFE)

◁◆▷

December 8, 1941

The Dock is crowded with men in military uniforms. We've scrubbed off the dirt of basic training, and now, we aim to eat, drink, and be merry. Every time the door opens, letting in a blast of snow and wind, we shout at the interloper to "close up or fuck off."

"Hey, Blanchard!" Another Seaman, Samuel Campbell, waves me over. He's got a beer in one hand and a buxom blonde in the other. "Did you get orders yet?"

"Not yet," I reply, clinking glasses with him. "You?"

"Nah," he grunts. "I washed out. Medical." He takes a swig of his beer before rolling up his pant leg to show me the knotted, black stitches running down his calf. "The obstacle course kicked my ass."

"That's crummy," I reply. "What are you going to do now?"

Campbell shrugs. "Try again when I heal up, maybe."

Suddenly, someone near the bar claps his hands, drawing our attention. "Hey! *Hey!* The president is on television!"

The bartender turns up the black-and-white television; President Franklin Roosevelt speaks to Congress. "Yesterday, December 7, 1941 — a date which will live in infamy — the United States of America was suddenly and deliberately attacked by naval and air forces of the Empire of Japan," the president announces.

"Fuck," Campbell says, rising from his chair for a better view.

The entire bar remains quiet for six entire minutes. In six minutes, FDR tells us we are unequivocally at war. He says over two thousand Americans have died in an organized attack.

When the speech is over, and the broadcast has ended, there's a cacophony of curses. Some curse themselves. Others curse the Japanese. All are met with sympathetic nods and pats on the back.

"I didn't sign up for *war*," a man, still in his uniform, laments.

"My cousin is stationed at Pearl Harbor," another whispers.

"Maybe they'll have to take me now," Campbell says. "I would very much like to do some killing." I give him a sidelong look, expecting to see something akin to mirth in his eyes. Surely, he's joking. But instead, there's something else entirely: hunger.

"Samuel," I admonish him.

"What? They killed ours, didn't they?" He raises his eyebrows. "I think a little revenge is warranted, don't you?"

"I don't remember 'revenge' being a core value," I snort.

Samuel finishes the last of his beer, gulping down the froth. His Adam's apple bobs. "Survival of the fittest, pally," he says, slapping me on the back. "Survival of the fucking fittest. I'm heading out, see you around."

Later, I walk down Main toward my apartment, humming *I Don't Want To Set The World On Fire* under my breath. When I veer into the alley, I pause. It feels as though someone is watching me, hidden amidst the shadows. I inhale, but my human nose is easily confused by the odor of the nearby dumpster, the cooking smells emanating through my neighbors' vents.

Cautious, I continue my walk. Midway down the alley, something strikes me in the shoulder, spinning me on my heel. It's a giant, hulking wolf, its breath stinking. I look up into its eyes, a deep golden brown. "You're barking up the wrong fucking tree," I tell it.

Its ears flatten back against its skull. It's not entirely sure what to make of me. I know what it expected: fear, pants-wetting, inconsolable fear. But I'm an Alpha, and I'm unafraid. It pulls its lips away from its teeth, snarling. "Run," it growls.

"You first."

The wolf grasps me by the throat, lifting me up off of the ground. Its mouth opens wide, as if planning to swallow me whole. But then, I am suddenly far too heavy, all sharp points and fur. Wolfish, I outweigh my adversary by at least one hundred pounds, and I'm a head taller. It lunges, but I grasp its snout, giving it a good shake. "Submit," I say.

It boxes my ears, and I wince at the loud ringing that follows suit. Taking advantage of my distraction, the other wolf grasps my neck with its jaws, squeezing tight. The periphery of my vision goes black when I can't get any oxygen. For a brief moment, panic sets in. It's a residual fear, a product of my most basic instincts: flight or fight.

Right now, my body isn't able to do either, *I can't breathe!*

The wolf's jaws continue to tighten. My nostrils flare, each breath a wheeze. Then, I rake my claws down my opponent's face. I aim for its eyes. *Yip!* It releases me, and I inhale. *Breathe, breathe, yes, yes, you can breathe.*

Now. Kill him.

I leap atop my adversary, slamming the back of its skull against the asphalt with a sickening *thwump.* "Who are you?" I snarl.

It blinks up at me, not comprehending. I've stunned it. "Who are you?" I repeat.

Instead of speaking, its fur melts away. The face looking up at me is familiar. After all, I saw him at the bar mere moments ago. "Hey, pally," Samuel Campbell groans.

Samuel takes the proffered cup of Joe and sips it. He's wearing one of my outfits; both the slacks and shirt are too large for him. He looks like a kid playing dress up in his older brother's closet. "I didn't know there were any of *us* in Wharton," he says.

"There are a few," I reply, sitting. "My brother and his wife: Elton and Margaret. A woman named Flora. A young boy, no older than fourteen: Nicolas." I cup my own mug of coffee, warming my hands against the porcelain.

"It was a shock to find out my dinner was a *wolf*." Samuel laughs as though it's the funniest thing in the world. I find myself disgusted by it. I've never eaten a human—not once.

"Oh? What if I hadn't been?" I ask.

Samuel pats his belly, licking his lips. "Well, we certainly wouldn't be having this conversation," he adds, just in case the pantomime wasn't quite enough.

"We don't eat humans in Wharton," I say sternly. "If you're staying, you won't, either."

"Haven't you tried it?" Samuel asks, resting his elbows on his knees, surveying me with wide eyes.

"No," I say defensively. "Never."

"You're missing out," he replies. "It's like the fattiest, most tender pork roast you've ever eaten. It's hot—piping hot, as if it just came from the oven. Fear makes them warm, you know."

His description makes my mouth water. Despite myself, I lean forward, desperate to hear more. At the same time, I feel ill. *This is barbaric*. It's like I'm standing on the edge of a precipice. The ground feels very far away.

Samuel continues, "I once caught this girl. She got herself so worked up her blood was *pumping*. Every bite was soaked in it. It may as well have been a stew."

"Stop it!" I snap, the words ringing between us.

"You should really try it," Samuel says, undeterred. He takes a prolonged sip of his coffee, raising his eyebrows at me over the rim of his cup.

"We don't eat humans in Wharton," I insist. "If you are planning to live here, you've got to abide by the rules. Or, you can move on." Saliva drips down my throat, and I swallow, swallow, swallow. *Stop thinking about it*.

Samuel places his cup at his feet, resting his head on the back of the couch. He looks up at the ceiling, his eyes half-lidded. For a long moment, he's quiet. I start to wonder if he's fallen asleep. Then, he stretches like a cat in the sunshine. "I do like it here," he admits. "You know, this was just supposed to be a stop on my way back to Tennessee." He presses his lips together. "It would be nice to have a pack, even for a few weeks."

CHAPTER 22
(AMA)

The girl is taken from the shed in the early hours. It's akin to a funeral procession: Rafe and Elton, carrying the dinghy between them; Flora and I bringing up the rear carrying the oars. I catch a brief glimpse of her, wrapped in bed linen, on the floor of the dinghy as the two men pile in. We hand them the oars; the engine is too loud and will draw unwanted attention.

"This feels wrong," I whisper to Flora, as we watch the men grow out past the tetrapods. They gently lower her into the still, dark water.

She grasps my hand, giving it a gentle squeeze. "I know," she murmurs. "But we can't leave her where she was. Not if—" She trails off, but I know what she's thinking. *Not if we think Samuel killed her.* And, I suppose that's what we think. Except—

I'm still not sure.

When the dinghy returns to shore some minutes later, Rafe leaps out, dragging it up onto the sand. "Let's go," he says, uneasy. He doesn't want us to be caught. It's a dark night, and the moon is only a sliver, but we are exposed here.

"Shouldn't we say a few words?" Flora asks meekly.

"What could we possibly say?" Elton huffs.

I shift from one foot to another. My heels slide into and out of the displacing sand. I feel off-balance. "Maybe," I say slowly. "We could say something kind. Like: 'we hope you find peace.'"

"There," Elton snaps. "You've said it. Let's go before the black-and-whites show up."

Rafe nods, but he offers me a tight smile.

As the four of us walk back toward the motel, Rafe drapes his free arm around my waist, pressing his lips against the side of my head. It's the first intimate touch we've exchanged since this morning. It makes me feel better.

Flora notices and squeaks. She claps her hand over her mouth—we're supposed to be quiet. Through her fingers, she whispers, "You two!" She nearly bounds through the sand and throws her arms around me. "I *love* this for you—both of you."

"We just did a truly terrible thing," Rafe snaps. "Can we not do this right now?" The men lug the dingy back into the shed, and I try very hard not to look at its open door. I fear that, somehow, the girl will have found her way back, her hair sopping wet and crabs pouring out of her mouth.

"Sorry," Flora mutters. But she beams at me, not entirely undeterred. When we reach the motel parking lot and kick the sand off our shoes, she squeezes my hand one last time. "I'm coming over later," she promises. Flora heads toward the front office, to relieve Mags who has been watching the desk in her stead.

Elton lights a cigarette, waiting for his wife. When Mags appears in the doorway, he flicks a bit of ash onto the asphalt. "We have to deal with Samuel," he grunts.

"I know," Rafe replies.

I look sharply between the two men. "Neither of you were in that shed. He seemed so upset."

"Maybe he was upset because his prey got discovered," Elton snorts.

Mags, reaching us, takes the cigarette from her husband. "Samuel left soon after you did," she says. "He needed to take a walk, he said."

"Great." Elton rolls his eyes. "There'll be another body in the morning."

There are two girls on the beach, their fingers interlocked. Neither look at me. Instead, they look toward the ocean. The waves slowly roll toward the shore, erasing any imperfection on the sand. The moon is full, making the sand appear silvery.

They dig their toes into the cool sand there, looking down at the slightly lucent surface. They don't seem to notice me as I approach. That's when I hear it: the crunch of splintering bone, the grinding of joints, a wet, rattling breath. Both girls crumple into a heap.

I wake with a gasp, my chest heaving. The light filtering through the windows is gray; it's nearly dawn.

"Bad dream?" Rafe asks sleepily. He wraps his arms around me.

"I can't stop thinking about them," I murmur, wiping sudden tears from my eyes. "It's as though they are haunting me. Do I sound nuts?"

Rafe props himself up onto his elbow, looking down at me. "No, not at all." He strokes my cheek with his calloused thumb. "I've experienced that too—I still do."

"Really?"

Rafe presses his lips together, not quite looking at me. "I've never told anyone about this. I see a dead man, too."

I want to touch him, but I'm afraid he will disappear before my eyes. He seems so fragile, incorporeal. He glances up at the corner of my room, grimacing. "I see him all of the time," he continues slowly, "because I'm the reason he died."

I wait with bated breath.

"His name is—was—Vincent. He was an ensign on my boat. Young, barely eighteen, if that. I was a gunner, and it was also my job to protect the ammo. The enemy would often sneak aboard and steal it, or tamper with it." Rafe lays back down beside me, his breath hot on my neck. When he speaks, he wets my skin.

"One night, I heard someone on the deck, and I crept out of the castemate to confront them. It was dark, and no one usually patrols there—not at that time of night. But there was a man there. When I shouted for him to announce himself, he stepped back into the shadows. So, I shot him."

Rafe strokes my naked flesh as he speaks, running his hands over my flat belly and the curve of my hip. "When I approached him, I saw it wasn't a Japanese saboteur at all. It was Vincent, and he was bleeding out. I got him in the shoulder, and there was just a *hole* there. I couldn't stop the bleeding, and he died within a few minutes."

"Oh, Rafe." I stroke his hair. "It sounds like it was an accident." The memory clearly tortures him. His skin thrums beneath my fingertips.

"Yes. But what happened afterward wasn't." He swallows hard, coughs once. It's as though the memory is a mass in his throat, around which his voice must crackle.

"I knew that I should wake someone, report what happened. But instead, I had a taste." Abruptly, he sits up, the blankets pooling around his waist. His spine curves like a parenthesis. "He was in my lap, and I was covered in his blood. I put one of his fingers in my mouth."

I'm afraid to move. *I'm afraid.*

"Before I knew it, I was wolfish, and I took a bite. Just one bite. I swear, Ama, it was just one," he continues. "Then, I pushed him overboard." His eyes meet mine.

I can't help but picture Rafe's jaws sinking into the belly of the girl in the dunes, shaking the life from her. I can't help but imagine him hiding the girl in the shed, just like the ensign he cast into the sea. Could he have done all of this?

Rafe rises from my bed, pulling his clothes on. He's interpreted my silence as horror, and he's not entirely wrong. He doesn't look at me as he dresses, nor does he say a word. In the grey light, he looks amorphous. It's as though he's mid-transformation when the body is weakest.

"Rafe," I manage, but my voice sounds wrong—stilted.

"I'm going home," he says. "I can't be here, not with you looking at me like that."

CHAPTER 23
(RAFE)

⊲◆⊳

The alcohol burns as I pour it down my throat. I had hoped it would quiet the churning in my belly, but instead, it sloshes therein. I feel sick. I keep thinking I see the ensign out of the corner of my eye, but when I turn to look, there's no one there.

I am midway through the bottle when my legs give way. I crawl to the toilet, my guts spilling into the bowl as I heave. Ama's eyes—I can't stop thinking of Ama's eyes. She looked at me as though I was grotesque. A monster. But aren't I?

Suddenly, my phone rings. I groan, wiping the spittle from my mouth. When it finally quiets, I sigh in relief. I'm not in the mood to speak to anyone. But then, it starts again. I wrench the receiver off of the cradle. "What?"

The line crackles. "Rafe?" Despite the slight tinniness, I recognize the voice.

"Samuel?" None of us have heard from him since the girl was discovered. Elton even walked past his rat-trap apartment and found neither hide nor hair of him.

"Come to the water tower," he pants. "Please." He sounds harried.

"Where are you?" I attempt to sit on the edge of my bed, but instead, I slide to the floor with a thump. I'm very drunk.

"Payphone outside of The Dock. The water tower, Rafe, please." I imagine him sitting in the cramped phone alcove just outside the entrance, huddling over the dog-eared phone book. There's graffiti inside the alcove: a drawing of Kilroy, his bulbous nose peeking over a rudimentary wall, a smattering of phone numbers, and a rude depiction of a penis.

"Fine," I relent. "Give me twenty minutes." After hanging up, I rest my forehead on my knees. The room tilt-shifts. I desperately wanted to say no, but Samuel is reaching out; he may have something important to say. He may confess.

I briefly close my eyes, trying to will myself into some semblance of sobriety.

He didn't do it, the ensign says, breathing into my ear. *Maybe you did—maybe you just don't remember.*

I scoff. "I didn't." My voice is loud in the quiet room. Of course, I'm speaking to myself. I'm the only one here. "I would know if I had, wouldn't I?"

♦ ♦ ♦

Samuel leans against a concrete pylon, his arms crossed over his chest. When I crest the hill, he stands up straight. His clothes are wrinkled; brown patches stain his knees where he'd kneeled in the girl's blood. His hair, often coiffed into a greasy pompadour, is in his face, curling around his ears. "I didn't do it," he says without preamble.

"Who else could it have been, Sam?" I ask, wary. "The thing is: you have a history. We both know it."

"I'm not that guy anymore," Samuel insists.

"Well, enlighten me," I say. "What sort of guy are you?"

Samuel spits on the ground. "Not the sort that murders a girl and leaves her at my fucking workplace." He scoffs. "I'm not a meatball." He reaches into his pocket for a pack of cigarettes, selecting one. "I never leave evidence behind." The strike of the match reveals his features in stark relief. Samuel looks as though he hasn't slept since the day before. There are deep, gray circles under his bloodshot eyes. His skin is oily, and a pimple has erupted on his jaw.

He offers me a cigarette and lights it for me. "I think," he continues, "it was Elton."

Elton?

"That's my brother you're talking about," I say in warning. "He would never."

"He's been conspicuously absent," Samuel says, shrugging his slender shoulders, "when these things have happened."

"He has a family."

"We all have families." Samuel takes a drag of his cigarette, the smoke trickling from his pursed lips. "You weren't here last summer. He was running the motel—the pack—with an iron fist. That tiny modicum of power made him horrific to be around. But he was always late to his shifts, lied to Mags, terrorized Nico and Flora, and would disappear for days at a time. He changed his tune as soon as you arrived at port."

"This is ridiculous." Samuel sounds delusional. He's grasping for anything to scrabble out of the pit he dug himself.

"Talk to the girls," Samuel says, flicking ash into the air. "Or, you can wait for it to happen again. He won't be able to help himself." He reaches behind the pylon, picking up a jacket and a small suitcase. "I'm heading back to Tennessee, but," he says, "I wanted you to know...I didn't break my promise."

I think of the night Samuel and I sat in my living room. We were both panting, shaken from our encounter in the alleyway. Neither of us wanted to admit to it. When I asked him to stay, he looked at me with dark eyes. *I've never had a pack*, he'd said, chewing on the words. *I'll stay. I promise, I'll do right by you.*

"Good bye, Rafe," Samuel says. "Tell Ama goodbye for me. She was always kind. Flora, too."

I think of grasping his arm, hauling him back toward the motel. But I've been broadsided. The ground rocks under my feet, and for a moment, it's like being back on the deck of the *West Virginia*. I watch him pick his way down the hillside toward the edge of town, and beyond it—the bus depot. He turns back midway down Elm, and, while he surely can't see me on the hilltop, he waves anyway.

I think it was Elton. The words coil around my skull, squeezing tight. Or is that the impending hangover? I stumble home, hoping the walk will untangle the knot inside of me. Instead, I enter my apartment all the more bound. *I think it was Elton. I think it was Elton. I think it was Elton.*

CHAPTER 24
(AMA)

◁◆▷

It is hot on the breezeway and in the guest rooms. I pull the polyester of my dress away from my armpits when no one is looking, hoping a breeze will quiet my perspiring skin. But it's all for naught. There's no power in the motel today, and there's no relief. Flora peeks into Room Seven, knocking on the doorjamb with her knuckles. "Elton says the whole block is down."

"Great." I sigh. I brush my hair out of my face, grimacing when it sticks to my sweaty forehead. "The guests will be miserable."

"*We're* going to be miserable," Flora corrects me. "At least the guests can go in the pool."

I chuckle, reaching down to pick up a candy wrapper a guest had left on the carpet. "Lucky them. Say, have you seen Rafe today?"

"Sure have," Flora says, waggling her eyebrows at me. "He's around here somewhere."

As if summoned, Rafe appears in the doorway, looking at the two of us with something akin to disdain. "Less chatting, more working." He scowls.

"Someone's in a foul mood," Flora observes, but she heads back to the Front Office regardless.

"Rafe," I sputter when he shifts as if to leave. "Please. Wait." His eyes are smoldering, dark coals. His lips press into a firm line. But he lingers. "I want to talk."

"About?" I notice then he is still wearing the clothes he left my bungalow in. He looks rumpled, his hair mussed on one side.

"Last night," I reply, stepping toward him, taking his hand. "Rafe, you shouldn't have left." His face, so stalwart, doesn't change. His lip, however, trembles. It would be imperceptible if I wasn't standing so close. "You're not a bad man," I continue.

"I did a horrible thing," he murmurs.

"I know," I whisper, reaching up and touching his cheek. "But Rafe—" I pause, unsure how to verbalize what I've been longing to say. "But that's not who you are. I think that I—"

He looks down at me, his breath hot and reeking of alcohol. "Ama," he says, a warning implicit therein. *Don't you dare.*

"I think that I love you," I finish, undeterred. He wavers in the doorway, neither coming nor going, his eyes boring into mine. Behind him, a gaggle of guests wander past, dressed in beachwear.

One pauses, making eye contact with me. "Can we get more towels in Ten?" he asks.

"Sure," I say. "I'll get right on that." Rafe doesn't acknowledge the guests at all, waiting for them to continue on their way. "Rafe," I say slowly when they are out of earshot. "Did you hear me? I said—"

"I heard what you said." He steps into the room, and I take a step back so we don't collide. He shuts the door. Immediately, it's as though the temperature rises. The air isn't circulating, and it's like breathing in soup. A trickle of sweat edges down my collarbone between my breasts.

Without warning, his mouth presses against mine. Our teeth clack together. His calloused hands cup my face. I press my tongue into his hot mouth, tasting bourbon and toothpaste. I rest my palms against his chest, his heart pounding beneath my fingertips. I'm wearing a dress with a zipper beneath the armpit, and he unzips it with nimble fingers. It ends just above the jut of my hip, and he lets the fabric gape open, revealing my brassiere. He grips my breast through the thin fabric, his thumb encircling the hardening nipple.

"Rafe," I murmur into his mouth.

"Hush, Ama." He kisses my throat, tasting my salty flesh with the flat of his tongue. I mewl, wrinkling his shirt all the more with my fists.

With our bodies pressed together, it is sweltering. But Rafe doesn't seem to mind. In fact, he seems to relish in it. He sucks at my skin like I'm all the sustenance he needs. He pulls the cups of my brassiere up above my breasts, so he can take me in his hands.

He pulls my dress down my hips, and I step out of the circle of fabric. In just my underclothes, I feel slightly cooler. Rafe unhooks my bra, dipping his head to suck my nipple into his mouth, probing with the edge of his teeth. I undo the buttons on his shirt with shaking fingers, revealing his undershirt beneath.

Rafe walks me backward, and I expect for the bed to collide with the back of my knees. But instead, we step around the bed and into the dark bathroom. We break apart. Rafe starts removing his clothes. I pant, leaning back against the sink.

Naked, Rafe reaches behind the curtain of the bathtub, turning on the shower head. Then, he closes the distance between us again, his mouth finding mine. His teeth, suddenly sharp, drag along my lower lip making me gasp. Heat pools in my core, and I ache for him to slide his hand between my legs.

Deftly, Rafe lifts me up onto the countertop, stepping between my legs. The sound of the shower fills my ears. Why had he turned it on? His cock, thick and vascular, probes between my folds. When he enters me, he sinks his wolfish teeth into my shoulder. The pain is like a lance, but there's a warmth that follows that is akin to pleasure. *God.*

I run my palms down his spine, the muscles contorting under my touch. "You feel so good," Rafe groans, thrusting into me so hard my butt bumps against the sink faucet. His hands rest on my thighs, his nails dimpling my flesh just slightly.

We are both soaked in sweat. Our bodies become slippery with it. I wrap my arms tight around his neck, encouraging him onward. *More, deeper, harder!* Instead, he lifts me off the counter, stepping into the shower.

The water is so cold it's like a slap. I gasp, my nipples prickling painfully. The finger waves I had painstakingly made in my hair fall flat as soon as they are moistened. "Rafe!" I exclaim.

"You were hot, weren't you?" he asks, his smile impish.

He strokes his cock, his knuckles butting up against my thigh. I reach down to replace his hand with mine, running my thumb over his bulbous head. Slowly, I ease down onto my knees in the bathtub, taking him into my mouth. His broad shoulders keep the water at bay, and when I look up at him, tiny rivulets of icy cold water trickle down his muscular chest. They make his pink nipples hard.

"You feel so good," Rafe croons, cupping my head with his hand. He presses his hips against my lips, the head of his cock edging against my soft palate. Suddenly, he urges me to my feet, his tongue circling mine. He presses me into the tile, his hand finally slipping between my thighs. When he finds the sensitive nub therein, I moan, tangling my fingers into his hair.

Just before he finally drives me to orgasm, he says, "I love you too."

Rafe and I lay naked on the bed in Room Seven, staring at the still ceiling fan. Our bodies are moist, and our limbs slip and slide against one another when we lean in to kiss, to touch, to nuzzle. We haven't spoken aloud since he said, *I love you, too*. I don't want to break the spell. Not yet.

Finally, he sighs. "I think you might be right about Samuel."

"Really?" I sit up, looking down at him. It's a surprise to hear him say that. He seemed so certain.

"I spoke to Sam last night. He...accused someone else in the pack." Rafe reaches up and strokes my side, trailing the hollows of my ribs with his fingers.

"Who?"

Rafe shakes his head. "It was baseless. But it did make me think. Maybe we are looking in the wrong direction."

I am suddenly imbued with a sense of purpose, a manic energy fizzling through each of my fingers. I want to help the victims find peace. Maybe then, maybe *they* won't appear in my dreams. Maybe I'll be able to take a single breath without thinking of them. "Let's talk to Samuel. Perhaps the three of us—"

Rafe holds up a hand to silence me. "Samuel is gone. I watched him go to the bus depot. He should be halfway to Tennessee by now."

"But we need him."

"We don't," Rafe insists. "Come here, wolf-girl." He pulls me down atop him, making me squeak in surprise. "Is it true?" he asks, breathy.

"Is what true?" I ask, perplexed.

"That you love me?" A grin flickers on his lips, as he tries, in vain, to hide it. He just wants to hear me say it.

"Yes, Mr. Blanchard," I coo. "I love you." The power suddenly comes on, the ceiling fan above our heads beginning to turn.

CHAPTER 25
(ELTON)

◁◆▷

I t was stupid to leave the girl in the shed.
But I was reckless. I saw her bobbing in the pool, her breasts pressed against a boogie board, and I could only think about how she might taste. When she asked me for another boogie board for her friend, I believed it was kismet. *Sure thing*, I'd said, leading her to the shed. *We've got plenty.*

Before I could finish, I heard Samuel coming, and I stuffed her beneath the detritus in the shed. It wouldn't do to have him discover her. I thought—incorrectly— that she was dead. Surely, she couldn't be alive after what I had done! But somehow, she found the strength to speak, to call for help.

Stupid. *Stupid.* I was nearly caught.

Tonight, I resolve to do better. I briefly consider abstaining altogether. Surely, I can do that! But the cravings keep me up, rolling around my stomach with a pronounced gurgle. I feared Mags would hear it, that it would rouse her from sleep.

I lay still for a long time, staring up at the ceiling. The ceiling fan spins, the breeze from its blades ruffling my hair. Mags mumbles beside me, nuzzling close. When we sleep, she is always touching me: a hand starfished on my soft belly, her chin tucked in my armpit, and a leg slung over mine. It's a comfort thing, not unlike the babies nursing even when they had no appetite. Typically, I enjoy it, but tonight, my skin is crawling.

I slowly get out of bed, careful not to wake her. I pad into the bathroom, switching on the light. Leaning heavily against the sink, I stare into the mirror. I nearly don't recognize myself. I'm sweating profusely, my pupils dilated. "Fuck," I grumble, to no one. I feel as though bugs are crawling all over my skin, in and out of my pajamas. I scratch at my flesh, leaving behind bloody craters.

I'm hungry.

I shouldn't do it again. I should crawl back into bed beside my wife. Maybe, when I wake up in the morning, I can muster a smile and help flip a pancake or two. I can bounce Carla on my knee and tell jokes. *Knock, knock.* But that's not what will happen, will it?

I've tried to abstain before. I'll sit up all night, staring at the wall until my eyes are dry and aching. I'll slouch through the day, bristly whenever the girls ask me to play. I'll become sick with need, excusing myself to the bathroom to dry heave and sweat. The phantom insects crawling across my skin will become all the more numerous, and I will scratch and scratch and scratch.

I dress quietly. *This will be the last time,* I tell myself.

♦ ♦ ♦

It's nearing midnight, and the streets of Wharton are quiet. The only people on the sidewalk reek of booze and stale sweat. They are clumped together in small flocks; it'll be difficult to separate one victim from the milieu. So I continue onward, heading down toward the pier. I light a cigarette, the smoke intermingling with the twinkle lights crisscrossing above. It's a romantic spot. I proposed to Mags here. I killed that girl—what was her name?—here, too, just beneath these floorboards. The pier is dotted with couples, taking advantage of the darkness to kiss, fondle, murmur sweet nothings.

I take the steps to the beach. Tilting my chin toward the heavens, nostrils flaring, I search for my fix. At first, I only inhale the piquant aroma of the beach: the brackish sea air, sulfurous algae blooms floating atop the rolling waves, and the decomposition of plant and animal life.

But then, I smell it. I follow the odor, tugging at it like a fishing line. As I walk it becomes stronger, so I walk faster. Then, I break into a trot, casting my gaze left and right. *Where is it coming from?*

I find myself walking abreast of the Cove Motel, the squat building on my right. The beach becomes less hospitable here: boulders and dunes shaggy with sea grass, keeping the summer set away. The smell grows stronger as I approach a cluster of boulders. Then, I see them: two men, sitting side by side. They pass a tightly rolled joint back and forth. The woodsy smell of marijuana makes me feel heady.

"I should be heading home," one of the men say.

"Stay a little longer," the other replies. There's something familiar about this voice, but with the perpetual undulation of the ocean, I can't quite hear it well enough to make heads nor tails of it. Perhaps he is a local, one of the dozens I interact with day-to-day. I prefer tourists to locals, but they both smell so *appetizing*.

"I can stay for a few more minutes," the man relents, leaning close to his companion.

I slowly edge around the boulders, my hands in my pockets. Saliva pools in my mouth, so much so that it trickles from the corners of my mouth. My skin crawls and itches, charcoal-colored fur popping out of my pores. My stomach clenches tight, then releases like a sigh. I leap atop the boulder, knocking one of the men to the sand below.

The other turns toward me in surprise, and I sink my teeth into the flesh just beneath the curve of his rib. Blood spurts into my mouth and I swallow the thick liquid over and over.

The man's knuckles connect with my snout, but it barely registers. Then, he calls my name. "Elton!"

Wait, no. Please, no.

I release the man, rearing back. Nico looks up at me with wide eyes. He presses his palms against the wound, his teeth chattering. He's in shock, his face nearly as pale as the moon above. "Elton," he manages through trembling lips.

I cup the younger man's face in my wolfish hands. His blood is salty in my mouth, and I hate that my body craves more, more, *more*. I want to throw it all up, turn

171

myself inside out to rid myself of every ounce of him. I can't help but think of days before, when Nico stood in my living room, laughing as a child dangled from his bicep.

The girls called—call—him "uncle." I call him "son."

Oh, my boy. My poor, poor, boy.

"I'm sorry," I whisper, placing my hands over his.

But Nico kicks me with his foot, scrabbling out from beneath me. He regains his footing some distance away, swaying. I sit on my haunches, watching him as he stumbles away. The other man has already taken flight, running through the sand along the shoreline. I can just barely hear him weeping. I feel tethered to the spot. *What do I do?* I'm looking down the barrel of a gun now. No matter what I do, I'll die. If I kill Nico, I will succumb to heartbreak; it would be like killing my own child. If he survives, and reveals his attacker to the pack, my brother will hunt me doggedly.

What do I do?

CHAPTER 26
(RAFE)

◁◆▷

"This is it," I say, embarrassed.

Ama looks around my apartment, fingering the odds and ends on my shelves. Her lips part into a soft half-smile and she hums to herself, as if she's forgotten where she is, that she isn't alone. She admires a collection of bisque figurines, inherited from my mother: two Parisian dancers and a horse-drawn carriage. She spins a globe, her face inches from the surface so she can see the rivers, valleys, and mountains pass her by.

"I think it's lovely," she says, though I'm sure she's just being polite.

My apartment is a hodgepodge—odds and ends ferreted away to form a sort of nest. There's my mother's figurines, knickknacks from overseas, and a small library's worth of books. It's not that I'm a voracious reader. Rather, I have *aspirations* to be one.

At present, I'm simply a book collector.

"You're lovely," I say, coming up behind her, kissing the swanlike curve of her neck.

She bats me away, playful. "Surely, you didn't invite me over just to slide your hands inside my dress."

"I did plan on it, yes." I fiddle with the zipper of her dress, inching it down, tooth by tooth.

"You're insatiable." She laughs, but she doesn't stop me from pulling the zipper down. I did like taking this dress off of her this afternoon. I would definitely enjoy doing it again here in the air conditioning. But, as soon as I slip my paw inside her dress, there's a knock at the door.

"Just ignore it," I whisper into the curve of her ear.

Then, the door-knocker calls out, "Rafe! It's Nico! I need you."

"You should get that," Ama urges. With regret, I zip Ama back into her dress, planting a final kiss on her shoulder. She sits on the couch while I fetch Nico.

Nico is breathless and pale, his arms wrapped tight around his midsection. He looks as though he may vomit. "There was another attack," he says.

"What?"

Slowly, Nico pulls his arms away, and blood jettisons out of a bite in his side. I clap my hands over it as his legs buckle. "Who? Nico—can you hear me? Who did this?"

Ama rushes into the kitchen and the bathroom in turn, returning with an armful of towels. She drops the lot unceremoniously at my side before hurriedly opening cabinets and drawers. "A first aid kit," she says, "Rafe, where's the first aid kit?"

My Carlisle kit is in the office. I don't have anything here. I curse my lack of foresight.

"Just get more towels," I say, pressing more and more cloth against the wound. The blood soaks through. *Why can't I get it to stop?*

Nico's eyes flutter closed. I slap his cheeks. "Nicolas! Stay with me," I say through gritted teeth. "Who did this?"

Nico murmurs something I don't quite understand. I lean close, so my ear is nearly flush with his mouth. His lips are cracked and rough. "Eh—" He coughs.

"Who?" I plead. Ama brings me more towels, and I press them against his side. But it's pointless; I'm prolonging the inevitable. I can see the glistening curve of his intestine through the tear in his skin.

He lets out a rattling breath, and a name follows suit: "Elton."

Elton!

I feel sick. There's a large part of me that wants to recoil from my task and sink into myself, but Nico needs me to be stalwart. Nico needs me to hold his hand. He's so young. Surely, he's scared. I'm scared.

"Hold on," I tell him. "Let's call somebody."

Ama is already on the phone. I can't hear her. My heartbeat is pounding in my ears. The ensign stands in the corner of the room, standing at attention. I try very hard not to look at him. *You did this*, he hisses, his teeth as pointy as a viper's. *This is your fault.*

Nico's eyes close, and I can't cajole him into opening them again. His chest stills. A horrible keening noise fills the room, and it takes me a moment to realize it is coming from me.

Ama's hands—unearthly strong—pull me up and away from the dead boy. "Rafe, Rafe," she shouts over the din, "Rafe!" But I can't stop. Grief rolls around and through me. I'm not sure which element of it hurts most keenly: Nico's death or Elton's unthinkable act. Both pummel me like the ocean batters boats during a hurricane.

◆ ◆ ◆

I stare at the spot on the carpet where Nico had been. It's still damp, and a veritable mountain of soiled towels stands alongside. The paramedics and the police have come and gone. To them, the case is open and shut: Nico was attacked by a rabid dog in the alleyway behind my apartment. At least, that's what we told them. Ama made a big show of describing a mangy dog: its body covered in flea bites, its jaws runneth over with foam.

Ama brings me a cup of tea, setting it on the end table. Then, she sits beside me. She is pale, dark circles beneath her eyes. We've been up for hours speaking to police. "Drink up," she prompts.

Obediently, I take the cup into my hands, taking a small sip. The tea is fragrant—chamomile. I look down into the liquid, the dark tea leaves swirling at the bottom. If I am very still, the surface becomes a mirror, and I can see my pinched face.

"He says it was Elton," I whisper. *I can't believe it. My brother.*

"I know," Ama replies, resting her hand on my knee.

"I need to go to his house. I need to check on Mags—the kids. If he's rabid, I—" I trail off, my brain buzzing. I can't stop thinking of Nico's face, the way he looked up at me with those dead, glassy eyes. The same eyes the ensign had. The same eyes of a prey animal when it is caught between teeth or snare.

Abruptly, I rise, sloshing my tea. "I can't sit here."

"Well, I'm coming with you," Ama says, her voice firm. She is defiant and bristly, as if expecting me to say *no, you stay here*. But I'm secretly glad. Maybe if she's there, if she's watching, I won't do something I'll regret for the rest of my life.

CHAPTER 27
(AMA)

The younger Blanchard sibling lives in a small bungalow on the far side of Wharton. It backs up to the forest, rather than the ocean. Here, the breeze smells like pine rather than salt. It ruffles my hair as we walk up the driveway. Mosquitos alight on my arms, and I slap them away.

Rafe pauses just before the front porch, grasping my wrist. His hands are still covered in Nico's blood, though now, it is dry and flaky like rust. "Let me handle Elton," he says, his voice devoid of emotion.

"I will," I promise him.

The bungalow is quiet. The blinds are drawn, which is not unexpected; it's nearly 3 a.m. Rafe knocks on the door. There's movement inside: a shuffle, a cough, the sound of a throat clearing. Then, Mags opens the door. She's in a long nightgown, her hair braided over her shoulder. "Rafe? Ama?" she yawns. "What are you doing here? What time is it?"

"It's late," I say gently. "Margaret, is Elton here?"

Mags cocks her head. "He wasn't in bed. When I heard the door, I reached out to shake him awake, but his side of the bed was empty." Her eyes flick to her brother-in-law. He must be a sight: his shirt stained brown, his forearms and hands the same. He resembles a swamp monster, just having risen from the bog. "What's going on?"

Rafe presses past her, looking into each darkened bedroom. He is quiet, careful not to wake his slumbering nieces.

I propel Mags out onto the porch. "Mags," I say softly. "Nico is dead."

Mags' face, lit only by the porch light, transforms. She opens her mouth in a silent wail, her eyes crinkling as tears spring forth. "Nico!" she cries. "Oh god, Nicolas." She leans into me, slumping into my arms. I hold the larger woman close, her tears wetting my dress. "What happened?" she sobs.

"He said," I swallow, unsure. Changing course, I continue, "He was attacked. Bitten straight through his side. He lost too much blood."

"Attacked by what—who?"

"He said—"

"He said he was attacked by Elton," Rafe finishes, standing in the doorway. His voice is flat. "He's not here," he adds, the latter for me alone.

"Elton wouldn't do this," Mags says, turning to Rafe. "He wouldn't."

"Where did he go tonight, Margaret?" Rafe asks.

"I—I don't know. He was here when I went to sleep." She fiddles with her braid, contemplating.

"Sometimes, when he can't sleep, he likes to go for walks. Maybe he's out walking."

I feel so badly for her. She looks ripped in two: wanting to defend her husband but anguished over the death of her pack mate. "Mags," I say kindly. "Where does Elton like to walk?"

"The beach, I think," she manages, wracked with seemingly unending tears. She swipes at them with her palms, over and over.

Rafe is already sprouting fur. It makes him appear bearded. "I'll find him," he says before the metamorphosis doubles him over in pain. "Stay with Mags, Ama." Before I can argue, he's gone, loping into the tree line.

"Let's get you inside," I tell Mags, taking her arm. "I'll make you a cup of tea." I've been brewing a lot of tea tonight. I'm not sure why. It's nice to have something to do with my hands. Perhaps it reminds me of sick days home from school, the very few occasions where my father would make me breakfast and bring it to my bedside. There would always be a cup of luke-warm tea, steeped for far too long.

Mags allows me to lead her inside. Her home is very unlike Rafe's: it is untidy, ostensibly lived in. Children's toys litter the ground. I scoot a herd of marbles aside with my toe as I head into the kitchen. The kitchen has a large picture window. In the daytime, the room must be bright and airy. But, in the dark, it's hard not to feel like I'm being watched by the shadows shifting outside.

I find a teakettle and put water on to boil. Mags wanders in as if sleep-walking, her hands tucked into her armpits. For a long moment, she simply looks out the window, her own face reflecting back. "I can't believe this," she murmurs.

"I know." I prep the tea leaves. "Nico is—was— so young."

"Elton loved that boy," Mags says pointedly. "He was like a son."

I feel as though I'm stepping into dangerous territory. In a sense, I still feel like an alien in their world. I'm not in the pack so much as pack adjacent. I didn't know Nico well. "I'm sure Rafe will sort this out," I finally say.

The kettle whistles. I reach for it, but Mags suddenly grabs my wrist, squeezing tight. Her eyes are wide, wet with unshed tears. "It could have been Rafe," she exclaims, the words spilling out of her mouth.

"Rafe?" I reply dumbly. She's squeezing so tight. Her nails cut shallow half-moons into my flesh.

"Maybe he's done all of this. He left us, he came back an entirely different person," she continues. "Or maybe he didn't really go at all. Maybe, he was here *hunting*." She laughs, but the sound is devoid of joy or humor. "Maybe that's what happened."

The kettle keens.

"Mags," I manage. "The kettle—the girls will wake up." I know what she's doing. I did the same with Bernie: jumping for any conceivable foothold, hoping it will protect my heart. *If I can change everything about myself, then he will love me. If there is another suspect, a question unanswered, Elton will be innocent.*

I untangle my arm from her grasp, lifting the kettle off the burner. The room goes silent. We simply stare at one another. "Margaret," I finally whisper. "He couldn't have. He was with me when Nico was attacked."

"Elton wouldn't," Mags gasps. "Ama, not my Elton." Her breaths grow shallow and rapid as panic sets in.

"Breathe," I remind her. "Sit down." I help her into a chair at the table, then pour the hot water over the tea leaves. When I place the mug in front of her, she cups it with her shaking hands. But she doesn't drink.

"Mommy?" Mags' youngest daughter, Carla, stands in the doorway, a stuffed bear dangling from her hand.

Oh, Carla!" Mags rockets out of her chair, rushing to the small girl. "What are you doing out of bed?"

"I thought I heard Uncle Rafe," the little girl replies. "Why's Ms. Ama here?"

"Hi, Carla," I say. "Your mommy and I are just talking. Did we wake you?"

Carla shakes her head. "Mommy, can I have a glass of milk?"

"Sure, baby." Mags grabs the milk carton from the fridge, pouring her a half-glass. After the child drinks, Mags hustles her out of the room. "Now, back to bed."

Though out of sight, I can still hear them in the hall. "Where's daddy?" Carla asks. "I looked in your bed and nobody was there. Not you, not daddy—no one. I was scared."

"Daddy is out with Uncle Rafe," Mags says. "Let me tuck you in. That's it, get under the covers now. Mommy loves you." Mags returns with dry eyes and a thin mouth. She eases back into her seat. "I told him to stop."

"What?"

"I told Elton to stop." She sips her tea. "He told me—he said it was only those few times, it would never happen again."

"What are you talking about?" The hair on the back of my neck stands up, and a shiver courses down my spine. It's like I've fallen into a frozen lake, the ice shattering beneath me.

"Elton just wanted to try it—once. Just the once. But it got out of hand. He couldn't stop. I begged him—*pleaded*—but he felt untouchable. That's what eating them does to you. It makes you feel like you can do *anything*."

"Mags—" I sink into the seat opposite. "Are you saying he's the one killing those people?"

She nods. "But, *but*, he would never hurt Nico. Not *ever*."

Inwardly, I'm screaming for Rafe to return. I'm not sure what to do. So, I keep her talking. "Why didn't you tell anybody?" I ask.

She shakes her head. "He's been agitated, volatile. I didn't want him angry at me or the girls." She cranes her neck, staring down the dark hallway, eyeing the girls' closed door. It's as though she needs to reassure herself that they are still there, still safe.

"Did Nico know?"

"No," Mags says, running her hands over the convex surface of her cup. She absently traces the floral pattern and curlicues with shaking fingers. The tea is still warm, a trickle of steam curling just above the lip. "I don't think so. Only I knew."

"And," she continues, "Elton wouldn't hurt Nicolas, even if he had. Nico comes over and eats dinner every Friday, did you know that?"

I shake my head. But I can imagine them here at this very table: Elton, Mags, Nico, and the girls laughing, eating a meatloaf slathered in ketchup. Nico would scarf his food down, just like he did when sitting at the front desk in the motel. He always ate like it was his very last meal, like someone was going to take the plate away from him. I can even imagine Nico playing with the girls after dinner, letting them climb all over him as though he was a jungle gym. He was always helping the younger guests master the diving board or carrying them to and fro on his shoulders.

"I hope you're right," I finally say. "But someone hurt Nico, and we need to find out who."

CHAPTER 28
(RAFE)

——◁◆▷——

It is easy to find Elton's scent. It is an odor I associate with afternoons dozing on pool chairs; autumnal hunting trips, the air crisp; and the clinking of glasses over an abandoned game of gin rummy. I lose his scent near the water tower, and I spend a significant amount of time circling the pylons, nose to the ground. Then: *there!*

I follow him toward the beach. He meanders in the sand, walking in a zigzag as if searching for something. Then, only a few yards from the motel within a cloister of boulders, I find a smear of dried blood. I press my nose against the spot.

Nico.

They were both here when Nico was attacked. Someone else was too. An unfamiliar scent, thick with adrenaline, is on the rocks. I catch a whiff of cologne. It's the same scent I use: Alfred Dunhill toiletries. There was a third man here.

I try very hard to reconstruct the scene. Nico and the stranger were both here, sitting on one of the boulders. Then, Elton attacked, drawing blood *here*. The stranger must have ran then, heading toward the lights of Wharton. Perhaps he was running for help.

Elton followed him.

I expect to find a body within a few yards, but there's none there. I can see his deep heel-strikes in the sand, and following, Elton's paw prints. Clearly, Elton was toying with him. He loved to do that with prey. Often, he would slow down just enough for a deer to gain ten furloughs before speeding up and taking it down. I always wondered if it was to make it more challenging for himself. But maybe, it was to give the prey a little bit of hope before he sunk his teeth in.

I finally find Elton, naked, sitting in the sand. His mouth and chin are covered in blood. A supine body lays in the sand some distance away, a ragdoll. Elton doesn't acknowledge my presence. His elbows rest on his knees, casual. He may as well be holding a beer.

"What have you done?" I say gruffly. "Elton, what have you done?"

His shoulders rise and fall in a shrug. "I've been hunting." His voice sounds flat, impassive.

"You've been murdering innocent people," I amend.

"Samuel told me what it was like, and I thought 'he's pulling my leg.' But, it's *even better*. If you weren't so sanctimonious, I could show you. Then, you would understand."

"Elton, don't you realize what you've done? Nicolas is dead."

For the first time, Elton meets my eyes. His jaw is taut. "You're lying."

I turn my snout toward the body in the sand. "Nico was with that human on the rocks. He ran to my apartment afterward and died in my doorway." I sit back on my haunches, curling my tail around my paws.

Elton shakes his head. "It was just a human." But there's a quaver in his voice, a chink in his confidence.

"Nico is dead," I repeat slowly. "I held him in my arms."

Elton lurches to his feet, his buttocks coated in sand. "No," he whimpers. "No, no, no. You're lying." He stands toe to toe with me, looking up into my eyes. Even in different forms, our eyes are the same: dense and depthless. While his eyes give nothing away, I know he is frightened. I am too.

"Don't be scared," I tell the ensign as the dock rocks beneath us. He's shivering, his teeth chattering; he's in shock. I hope he can't feel it. I want to run for help, but I fear that if I go, he'll die alone. I find myself stroking his hair. My mother used to do the same for me when I was sick. But Vincent isn't sick, is he? He's dying.

"I wouldn't lie to you," I tell my brother.

Elton's face contorts. His lips tremble. "It was an accident," he whispers. "Oh, Rafe..."

"I know," I say, because I do.

The pain he's feeling is immeasurable. It is akin to a muscle spasm ratcheting tighter and tighter until all that remains is a Gordian knot. It's the feeling of being cracked open, having one's innards scooped out, only to be discarded in the summer sun. Even in moments of pure bliss, rare as they are, it's as though you're stuck to the asphalt, every stride leaving behind flesh, sinew, and chunks of bone.

"This wouldn't have happened," Elton says slowly. "If you hadn't come home." He jabs me in the chest with his forefinger. I barely feel it through my thick undercoat. "The others would have followed me."

"You're delusional," I guffaw. "Fucking bonkers." I've heard tales of rabid wolves, driven insane by eating human meat. It's akin to eating a prion-infected deer. Gradually, the prions gnaw through the brain, tearing apart neural pathways until one cannot think, feel, or employ reason.

"Nico would still be alive," Elton continues, nostrils flaring. Fur sprouts on his chest, rippling down his stomach. Before he can transform any further, I bat him off his feet. I'm gentle, but he lands heavily on his side in the sand. *Oomph.*

But then, he launches himself at me, fully formed, driving his shoulder into my stomach.

We tussle, neither able to land any significant blows. I'm holding back. I don't want to hurt him. Conversely, he's slipshod, unable to judge the distance between us. His jaws snap at the air.

Elton shoves my snout into the sand with one huge paw. Granules fill my nose, my mouth, and sting my eyes. I blindly kick at him, one hindfoot making contact with his kidney.

Yip!

Elton bares his teeth, thick semi-translucent saliva dripping off of his canines. He pins his ears back against his skull. "It's my pack," he says in a guttural voice. "Mine."

"You're a murderer," I remind him. "You killed a packmate. Countless humans." Elton winces, and I take the opportunity to close my claws around his throat, giving him a violent shake.

"What are you going to do about it?" he says, when I release him. But before I can answer, he kicks me in the knee. The bone breaks with a sickening crunch.

CHAPTER 29
(ELTON)

I didn't kill Nico. *I didn't.*
Despite seeing what I had done, hearing Rafe say it aloud, I refuse to believe it. *It's a lie.* I'll go home, and he'll be sitting cross-legged in my living room, a bag of potato chips in his lap. He'll be laughing, his face lined with mirth. He was always laughing.

I cut across Main Street, heading west toward my cabin. A car easing through the intersection honks, fishtailing, nearly hitting me. But I don't slow down. I need to go home. I need to see Mags. I need her to quiet the screaming-raging-*hunger* inside of me. Surely, she can do that.

I imagine resting my large head on her lap, her fingers stroking my forehead. She would make my fur smooth, silky like a seal's. I can't tell her about Nico. The thought bubbles up and bursts, spreading poison through my body. Mags won't hold me if she knows. She will rip me asunder. Then what will I have?

Nothing. Just my hunger.

In a sense, the prospect is tantalizing. I can just run, eat, and let the last dregs of my humanity drain out. I can travel through the eastern seaboard, the wind at my back, razing towns as I go. I can become infamous: a storybook monster, a ghost haunting children at night—their parents, too.

Finally, I reach the forest and beyond it—*the cabin*. I slow to a walk, creeping down the gravel drive. I don't want to wake the girls. I can't help but think of the nighttime routine we performed hours earlier. They always brushed their teeth with too much toothpaste. It makes them appear rabid, their mouths foamy and dripping. Is that what I look like now? Is that the last thing Nico saw before he ran from me?

I skirt around the cabin, heading to the back door. More often than not, we leave it unlocked. Then, I smell her. Them. There's the familiar scent of my wife: the minty shampoo she favors, the sharp smell of Borax. But there's someone else, too. Someone who smells like perfume, but also like my brother. *Ama is here.*

Surely, she's poisoning Mags against me. *He's a murderer*, she'll say. But this isn't my fault. Not truly. This is Rafe's fault. He should have died overseas, like I'd hoped. Or, at least, he should have come home changed, made anew. He was always so fucking chivalrous, always doing the right thing. He always denied himself so much pleasure, and for what? Just to hold it over my head?

Your Alpha is home, he'd said.

I reach for the doorknob, turning it slowly. *I'm home, girls.*

CHAPTER 30
(AMA)

The clock in the kitchen ticks, ticks, ticks. Neither Mags nor I move from the table—a stalemate. "What about Parnell?" I ask. "The man who confessed?"

Mags shrugs despondently. "People confess to things they haven't done all of the time. Maybe he thought he would be famous—or infamous."

"Do you know him?" I ask.

"I've seen him around, same as anyone. Wharton is a small town." She pushes her cup of tea away, sitting back in her chair with her arms crossed. "Why are you still here?"

"Rafe told me to stay," I remind her. I wish I could go. I can't shake the feeling I'm intruding. But Rafe was insistent. "He should be back soon," I add, though I have no idea if it's true.

Suddenly, there's a rustling sound just outside the kitchen window. I turn to look, but it's difficult to see anything at all. I can only see our reflections, backlit by the kitchen light. I start to rise, but Mags reaches out and squeezes my wrist. "Don't," she warns, her voice low.

"Why?"

"If Elton has been hunting, he'll be dangerous," she says in a rush. "Sometimes, if I knew he was hunting, I would go sleep in the girls' room with the door locked, just to stay out of his way. Sit still."

I sink back into my chair. "What do you mean "dangerous?"" I ask, alarmed. She had said he was agitated—volatile, even. But dangerous is an entirely different thing altogether.

The knob on the back door jiggles. Mags violently shakes her head. "Be quiet," she hisses. When the door opens, a breeze wafts down the hall, ruffling our hair. Then, a large lumbering figure eases through the doorway, ducking to fit. It's Elton, wolfish. He sniffs the doorknob of the girls' room, but doesn't enter. Instead, he continues into the kitchen.

Like Mags said: I sit still. Unfortunately, this means I lose sight of him as soon as he passes through the threshold. He's behind me. I can smell him: wet, sulfurous, almondy. There's a coppery smell too. Elton is bleeding. His hot breath wets my neck as he leans close, sniffing my hair, the hollow of my clavicle.

Mags watches, her fists clenched on the tabletop. "Elton," she says meekly.

Elton's wedge-shaped head turns toward his wife. His fur brushes against my face. He and I are nearly cheek to cheek, his large paw slowly coming to rest on my opposite shoulder. One long, scythe-like nail digs into my skin. "Ama just came to say hello," she continues.

"Is that right?" Elton asks, his voice so deep it rattles through my chest cavity.

Mags' eyes dart to mine. She licks at her dry lips, trembling. "Yes, that's right. She probably should head home though, it's getting late. We lost track of time."

Elton huffs. "I think Ama should stay." His talon pierces my skin, a thin trickle of blood seeping into my dress. It hurts, but I don't dare cry out. *Be still, be still, be still*, I remind myself over and over.

His bones crunch, and slowly, the paw on my shoulder is replaced with a hand. His furry cheek becomes stubbly and rough. Elton spits a thick globule of blood and saliva out onto the tabletop. "I should be the one to tell her," he continues, "that Rafe is dead."

No.

"Oh Elton, you didn't," Mags groans.

"He was delusional — a danger to the pack," Elton says deridingly. "He had to be put down."

The room tilt-shifts. *No, no, no.* I swallow the hot bile rising in my throat. There's something else too: a churning anger radiating through my chest. It's akin to the feeling I felt when Bernie hit me but amplified tenfold.

My teeth grind together. "Fuck you," I blurt out.

Elton's grip on my shoulder tightens, his nails digging into the hollow beneath my clavicle. "It's for the greater good," he explains as though I'm a child. "He would have killed you. He would have killed us all."

I drive my elbow backward into his stomach, and surprised, he releases my shoulder. I lurch to my feet and turn to face him. He's far taller than I am, and I stare up into his face. He looks down at me, his lip twitching as though he's trying to contain a grin. "I'll kill you," I snarl.

"You're wracked with grief," he says coolly. "You aren't thinking clearly. Sit down, Ama."

I step into my fur in seconds, the snap of bone barely registering. We are now eye-to-eye. Before he can react, I shove him backward into the stove. He knocks over the kettle, and it falls to the ground with a hollow clang. Elton doubles over with laughter. "You stupid girl," he snickers. I hate that he can't even pretend to mourn his brother, to feel conflicted about his actions.

"You're a monster," I growl.

"I'm a hero," he counters. "I'm saving this pack. I'm saving *you*."

I launch myself at him, and he's wolfish before my fist connects with his chin. I drive his snout up and back, but he shakes me off easily. We tussle, and his teeth sink into my shoulder. I yelp as my skin tears. He tosses me backward onto the table, and the wooden legs give out beneath me.

Mags leaps up, skirting around the wreckage to hide in her daughters' room.

I regain my feet, but Elton is there, ready to toss me aside again. "I'll put you down too, you—" he growls, but I drive my shoulder into his belly, cutting him off. I sink my jaws into his hip, squeezing tight. His fur and blood fills my mouth. Did he taste Rafe, coppery and brackish? His muscle bunches beneath my teeth.

Elton grasps me by the scruff of my neck, tossing me backward. I land on my back on the linoleum, and he leaps on top of me. He's heavy, and his breath is hot and stinking. He curls his paws around my throat, squeezing tight. "This is how I should have killed him," he snarls. "Just like this." His grip tightens.

Black motes burst in front of my eyes. I gasp, my tongue lolling out. *He's going to kill me.* I'm going to die here on the kitchen floor.

Suddenly, the windowpane shatters. Glass rains down on us. Elton's grip loosens, and I take a deep breath. A large, hulking figure collides with Elton, tossing him off me like a ragdoll. It's a black wolf, its teeth bared.

CHAPTER 31
(RAFE)

I lay panting on the sand, the sea breeze ruffling my fur. It feels good, warm and comforting like a mother's tongue on my pelt. I long to close my eyes. Maybe if I fall asleep, it won't hurt so much. Maybe I'll wake up, *renewed*. Maybe this will be nothing more than a dream—a nightmare.

My brother left me for dead. I watched him go, loping up and cresting the horizon, heading toward the forest. He's going home. I think of his squat little house, the driveway I had driven up less than an hour ago. I think of Ama standing on his porch, her hand on Mags' arm. *Ama*.

Elton will kill her. The thought bubbles up, bursting upon what remains of my consciousness. *I can't go to sleep, or she'll die*. I roll onto my belly, groaning. I slowly regain my feet, my back leg dragging. I take a step, my legs shaking. I need to run. She will die if I don't run. I grit my teeth and break into a jog, dragging my ruined leg behind me. Each step is torture, but I can't stop. I won't stop.

Ama.

♦ ♦ ♦

Finally, I approach the house. I'm in shock. My teeth are chattering. But the pain is somewhere far away, nestled in my hindbrain. *I need to get inside.* I test the front door, but it's locked. I limp around the side of the building, heading toward the back. The light of the kitchen window slices across the back lawn, and I wince; it hurts my eyes.

A snarl rumbles through the glass, and I turn to see my brother straddling Ama, both wolves streaked with blood. Ama's mouth is agape, her eyes wide and rolling. She can't breathe. She claws at Elton's shoulders, leaving deep trenches of blood behind. I don't have time to reach the back door. She's dying.

I smash through the glass and into my brother, tossing him off of Ama. She gasps, gulping air. Her paws alight on her throat, palpating the flesh there. "Rafe!" she exclaims.

My brother snarls, coiling beneath me like a rattlesnake. He strikes at me with bared teeth, clamping down on my foreleg. He intends to break that one too. But I parry his attack, my knuckles glancing off his sensitive nose. Then, Ama is upon him too, biting at his side, his haunch, wherever she can sink her sharp teeth. Elton kicks her away.

When he's distracted, I close my jaws on his throat. It takes very little pressure to draw blood and only a little more to knick the jugular vein therein. My mouth floods with blood, piquant and metallic. It coats my tongue, dripping down my throat.

"Ra—" he rattles, but then, his breath hitches. He doesn't take another.

I release him, hot tears blinding me. My fur slides off, and I fall, my uninjured leg unable to support my weight. For a moment, the pain blinds me, deafening my ears. It's as though I'm swimming through sludge. Vaguely, I hear Ama talking to me, feel her cool hands touching my face. I wish I could understand what she's saying; it is just noise now, static. But her touch is like a lighthouse, leading me home.

In the ambulance, the ensign sits in the jump seat, his ankle resting upon his knee. He's wearing his dress uniform, his shoes spit-shined. I can see my own face reflected in them. Vincent's head tilts, giving me a sidelong look.

This will hurt terribly, he tells me. I can't discern whether he's referring to the pain in my leg or the loss of my brother. *But* he continues, *it will be alright. Don't give up the ship—not again. Fair winds, Rafe.*

When I blink, he's gone. There's just a paramedic sitting there now, checking my pulse.

III. 1949

CHAPTER 32
(AMA)

❧✦❧

The bungalow is full of light. With the windows open, the air, cooled by the ocean, sweeps in. Rafe sits on the deck, his leg propped up on a pile of throw pillows. His eyes are closed, his lips slightly parted; he's dozing. I kiss the whirl of hair at the crown of his head, setting a cup of coffee on the table beside him.

His eyelids crack open, looking at me through his dark, thick lashes. "Thank you," he murmurs.

A newspaper upon the table announces the Soviets have become the first nuclear superpower: "Truman Says Russia Set Off Atom Blast!" I carefully fold it and tuck it under my arm.

Rafe slept fitfully the night before. He cried for his brother but quieted when I pulled him against my bosom, stroking his hair. He didn't remember when he woke this morning, and I didn't remind him. It would only cause him pain, just like the newspaper's fear mongering.

"You're welcome," I say, sitting on the edge of his chaise lounge so I can kiss his lips. One of his large hands rests upon my thigh, his thumb drawing lazy circles beneath the hem of my skirt. "You must be feeling better," I remark. The healing process has been long and slow. He's needed several surgeries to recover from the so-called 'dog attack.'

"I have a very adept nurse," he says, leaning forward to capture my lips with his. "She's been taking care of all of my needs." His hand slides beneath my skirt.

"She sounds nice." I laugh.

"You would like her very much," he croons, fiddling with the hem of my underwear. A long finger slips under the gusset, stroking me.

I gasp, batting him away. "Everyone will be here soon!" I admonish him, leaning away to look into the house decked out for a party. There's a charcuterie board on the counter and a rack of lamb in the oven, the door slightly ajar. Steam curls out of the oven as though it is a dragon's maw.

"They can wait on the porch. Come here, love." He urges me onto his lap. I lace my arms around his neck, kissing his smooth forehead.

"You're meant to be resting. The doctor said—"

"I remember what the doctor said," Rafe says, clucking his tongue. He palms the back of my neck, pulling my face close. "Surely, I've rested enough." Both hands slide beneath my dress, cupping my ass and giving it a firm squeeze. I can't help but mewl into his mouth. "That's it," he murmurs, shifting the gusset of my underwear aside so that he can press a finger into my heat.

I unbutton his pants, my fingers trembling. His cock presses against the Y-fronts of his underwear, and I free it, running my hands up and down its length. Precum glistens upon the tip, and I smear it around his bulbous head. He gasps, biting at his lip, his eyes meeting mine. They are as dark as they've ever been, but I feel like I can swim in those depths; I know the way, and he will keep me safe. He slips another finger inside of me.

I scoot closer so his cock presses against my thigh. Rafe replaces his fingers with his thickness, pressing firmly into me. He grasps my hips, guiding me up and down. He grunts, his nostrils flaring. "You feel so good," he growls.

He feels good, too. Rafe dips his head to kiss my neck, my clavicle. He tugs down the bodice of my dress, kissing my breast through the silky fabric of my brassiere. His teeth scrape against my nipple.

The doorbell rings.

"Rafe," I mutter, my eyes half-lidded. "I have to get that." But my fingers are in his hair, urging him onward. Rafe's body tenses, and a low groan escapes his lips as he orgasms. Then, before I can rise, anxious about our guests, he circles the calloused pad of his thumb around my sensitive pink nub, making starbursts dazzle my eyes.

"There," he says as I rise, red-faced, adjusting my clothes. He grins up at me as he tucks himself back into his slacks. "Now, we can answer the door." With effort, Rafe clambers off of the lounger, reaching for a cane leaning against the deck rail. He kisses me as he limps past, heading toward the door.

The doorbell rings twice in quick succession, as if saying *hello, is anyone there?*

I snicker and edge around my slow-moving lover, reaching the door first. When I throw it open, I find Margaret, Flora, Delia, Carla, and, slouching behind them, Samuel. Flora presses a warm casserole dish into my hands. "What took so long?" she asks, "we've been waiting!"

"I just had to put a few final touches on the lamb," I say smoothly, hoping my appearance doesn't give away the fib. My face still feels hot, my lips tingling with Rafe's kisses. "Come in, come in!"

Rafe embraces his sister-in-law and gives his nieces satchels of chocolate-covered malted milk balls. Carla squeals in delight, popping a few into her mouth. Chocolate drool weeps out of the corners of her lips as she chews. "Thank you, Uncle Rafe!" He musses her hair.

I serve drinks: a Gin Rickey for Flora, and Sidecars for Samuel, Mags, and Rafe. I pour a half-glass of Coca-Cola for myself. "Sam," I say warmly, handing him his drink. "How's Tennessee?"

Samuel looks less greasy than usual, though as dour as ever. He has been writing us letters for months now, and we have sent our fair share in return. Moving away from Wharton has been good for him. He's a mechanic now and has found a little pack to call his own. He was very happy to tell us he's been exclusively hunting stag and fallow deer. *No men, no women, nada,* he'd written in his jaunty script, underlining each word as if to say *I'm serious*.

"Good, Ama, thank you," he says. "My old lady has been keepin' me busy." Samuel's letters surprised us, too. He married a human divorcee named Nadia who has encouraged him to open his own garage. "We just put a down payment on a garage out in Sevierville, plan t' be up an' running in 1950."

"That's fantastic," I reply. "I'm sorry Nadia couldn't make it. I would have loved to meet her."

"I'll bring her next time," he promises. "Or, y'all can come out and' stay with us."

Flora sips her drink. "Have you had a good birthday so far, Rafe?"

"It's been amazing," Rafe replies, flashing me a coy smile. "Ama has been spoiling me." I can't help but chuckle and try, in vain, to hide it under my palm.

Mags is quiet, watching her girls run around our living room. Delia stands on the hearth of the fireplace, ordering her sister to call her Queen Dee, The One True Ruler of Camelot. Rafe sits down beside his sister-in-law, tucking his cane beneath the ottoman.

He wraps his arm around Mags' shoulders. "How are you?" he murmurs. They have grown very close since Elton's death, both having a mountain of grief to climb. I don't want to eavesdrop, so I sit beside Flora.

My friend rests her chin on my shoulder, her lips nearly touching my earlobe as she shares a secret. "Did you tell him?"

"No," I hiss back. "I'm not sure when would be the right time."

"Ama!" she exclaims, forgetting to quiet her voice. I hush her, gripping her wrists tight and giving her a gentle shake. "Oops," she whispers.

"Flora is going to help me in the kitchen," I announce to the room, though no one appears to be listening. Teeth gritted, I pull the younger woman to her feet, corralling her into the kitchen away from prying eyes—and ears. "I know," I say when we are alone, the sounds of the party muted. "But *how*? How do I tell him?"

Flora takes a slice of salami off the charcuterie board, popping it into her painted mouth. "Tell him tonight," she offers.

"Tonight? You mean, *tonight* tonight?" I press my palms against my hot cheeks, my stomach tumbling. I've tried to tell Rafe for days, but it's never seemed like the right time. In truth, I worry he'll be unhappy. We've never discussed the prospect before. We hadn't even joked about it.

"Yes, tonight." Flora picks up the charcuterie board, pressing it into my hands. "But first, you've got guests to take care of and a party to host." I'm pleased that "tonight" is far off. Surely, the party will run late. Then, it'll be silly to tell him just before bed.

Perhaps tomorrow? *Yes, tomorrow sounds good.*

When we walk back into the living room, Flora claps her hands. "Alright, everyone!" she shouts. "Ama has an announcement to make!"

Flora!

She takes a cube of gruyere cheese off the charcuterie board and nibbles the corner. Her eyes meet mine, and she grins. "Tonight," she repeats. "Now."

All of the party guests—-Samuel, Rafe, Mags, even the girls—turn to survey me. I swallow, suddenly aware of a thick, firm lump therein. My tongue feels dry. For a brief moment, I wish I could simply float up through the ceiling and away from here. But then, I look at Rafe. He's looking at me with those dark, cavernous eyes, his lips parted just slightly. It's the same look he gives me when he wakes to find me beside him each morning.

"What?" I say, rolling onto my stomach and propping myself onto my elbows. Rafe's palm encircles the back of my head, pulling me just a tad closer to kiss my lips. He doesn't mind my morning breath, that my hair is sticking on end, that there's a crease in my cheek from my pillow.

"I'm just happy," he replies. His thumb brushes against my lower lip. "And," he amends, "lucky as hell."

I place the charcuterie board on the end table and wipe imaginary crumbs off my hands. The silence in the room is palpable. I worry that when I do speak, the words will get stuck, that they will just hang in the air, unheard.

"I'm pregnant," I finally say.

Rafe lurches to his feet, nearly leaping over the ottoman to reach me. "Are you serious?" he asks, breathless. I nod, and he throws his arms around me, squeezing tight. His body quakes—with excitement or terror, I can't discern. When he holds me at arm's length, I find that he is crying. Fat tears trickle down his cheeks, wetting his short beard. I reach up and wipe them away with my thumbs.

"Are you happy?" I ask.

"Are you?" he counters. I'm not sure how to answer the question. The realization was like a slap, spinning me off-balance. I haven't quite regained my footing.

"Scared," I admit. "But I'm happy."

Before I can ask him the question again, he crushes my mouth with his. He doesn't seem to care that we are in the middle of our living room, surrounded by guests.

"Gross," exclaims Carla.

We break apart, peals of laughter doubling us over. Samuel reaches around us to grab a cracker off of the charcuterie board. "Congratulations," he says, his mouth full.

"Dinner is ready by the way," Flora chirps, clearly pleased with her handiwork. She gives me a wink. "Come along, everyone. Ama put a lot of work into this lamb, and it smells *divine.*"

While the others file into the kitchen to heap their plates with fragrant meat, Rafe wraps an arm around my waist. "I am very happy," he says, his tone serious. He rests his palm on my still-flat stomach. "Ama, I'm ecstatic."

Later, when we lay together in bed, I marvel at the life I've carved out for myself here in Wharton. I arrived in this town road-weary, unsure whether I was coming or going. I was a woman caught between worlds, who was always told "no, not like that."

Wolfish, I was collared. Human, I was imprisoned. But now? *I'm free.*

I sit up, pulling the bedsheets off of Rafe. "Mmmm," he complains, dozing after several celebratory libations. He presses the heels of his hands against his eyes.

"I want to go for a run," I announce, pulling my nightdress up over my head. "Are you coming?" My vertebrae crackles.

"Always," he says, throwing his legs over the side of the bed, his impending hangover forgotten, or at least, temporarily sidelined. "Lead the way."

THE END

ACKNOWLEDGMENTS

I want to thank my family for buying me a word processor when I was in middle school; Carleigh, for everything and then some; Tatum West, for teaching me everything I know; Reddhott Covers, for this gorgeous cover; and the powerful, magical women at 4 Horsemen for believing in me and this story.

ABOUT THE AUTHOR
BEAU LAKE

Beau Lake is a tattooed, blue-haired, queer romance writer skulking around the mountains of Virginia. She is very happily married and lives with a menagerie of children (2), dogs (3), and plants.

Her current hobbies include digital art, social/animal activism, and screaming into the void. Mostly the latter. She is passionate about ending greyhound racing in the United States and worldwide, and shares her home with a retired racer named River. Other favorite activities include listening to true crime podcasts, staring at empty Word documents while having existential crises, and asking herself "What Would Stephen King Do?"

Beau writes both traditional and horror/supernatural LGBTQIA romance. Werewolves are her favorite because they have sharp teeth and even sharper personalities.

Some of her published work includes the well-received DC Pride series, co-written with Tatum West

(Proud, Out, and The Space Between Us). The Wolves of Wharton is her first supernatural series, with more to come!

She can be found online via Facebook, Twitter, or at authorbeaulake.com. She loves talking with readers and can be reached at authorbeaulake@gmail.com. Vegetarian recipes are also appreciated.

facebook.com/beau.lake.77
facebook.com/groups/1813967932089935
Twitter @beau__lake
beaulakebooks.com

OTHER BOOKS

Co-authored w/ Tatum West:
Proud, Out, The Space Between Us

BY BEAU LAKE:

The Beast Beside Me
The Beast Within Me
The Beast After Me
The Beast Like Me

4 Horsemen Publications

Romance

Emily Bunney
All or Nothing
All the Way
All She Needs
Having it All
All at Once
All Together
All for Her

Mimi Francis
Private Lives
Second Chances

Fantasy/Paranormal Romance

Blaise Ramsay
Through The Black Mirror
The City of Nightmares
The Astral Tower
The Lost Book of the Old Blood
Shadow of the Dark Witch
Chamber of the Dead God

Valerie Willis
Cedric: The Demonic Knight
Romasanta: Father of Werewolves
The Oracle: Keeper of the Gaea's Gate
Artemis: Eye of Gaea
King Incubus: A New Reign

J.M. Paquette
Klauden's Ring
Solyn's Body
The Inbetween
Hannah's Heart
Call Me Forth
Invite Me In

V.C. Willis
Prince's Priest
Priest's Assassin

Young Adult Fantasy

C.R. Rice
Denial
Anger
Bargaining
Depression
Acceptance

J.B. Moonstar
Russ and The Hidden Voice
Taylor and the Red Wolf Rescue
Jenna and the Legend of the White Wolf
Jenna and the Return of the White Wolf
Jan and the Chinese Crested Tern Rescue

4HorsemenPublications.com

www.ingramcontent.com/pod-product-compliance
Lightning Source LLC
Chambersburg PA
CBHW050321110726
47899CB00007B/2327